BADMAN

Pace Reid was determined to get back at the man who betrayed him and his gang of outlaws, but he had taken a bullet and now he was bleeding, weak and without a horse. And he had a bigger problem: Judge Parker's relentless marshal, Ruven Blood. With Blood on his trail it took every ounce of Reid's toughness to keep going, but when a badman like Reid was burning to carry out his own personal justice, not even Marshal Blood could stop him.

Books by C. H. Haseloff
in the Linford Western Library:

DEAD WOMAN'S TRAIL
A KILLER COMES TO SHILOH
RIDE SOUTH!
MARAUDER

C. H. HASELOFF

BADMAN

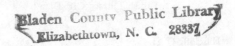
Complete and Unabridged

LINFORD
Leicester

First published in Great Britain in 1983 by
Bantam Books
London

First Linford Edition
published October 1995
by arrangement with
Bantam Books Inc
New York

British Library CIP Data

Haseloff, C. H.
    Badman.—Large print ed.—
Linford western library
I. Title II. Series
823.914 [F]

ISBN 0–7089–7763–4

Published by
F. A. Thorpe (Publishing) Ltd.
Anstey, Leicestershire

Set by Words & Graphics Ltd.
Anstey, Leicestershire
Printed and bound in Great Britain by
T. J. Press (Padstow) Ltd., Padstow, Cornwall

This book is printed on acid-free paper

To Dr. Henry B. Darling
with many thanks for his
encouragement
and to
Thomas J. Crowson
and
Guy Nichols
Fort Smith National Historic Site

1

November 15, 1888

PACE REID cut the switch lock and got ready to throw. The metal lever froze his rough bare hands. He cussed silently and jammed his red fingers deep into the pockets of his heavy wool coat.

Reid's job was to throw the switch and send the train onto a side track. It all seemed simple enough. Cut the lock; throw the switch. Bill Russell, Pood Ellis, Thom Roots, and Reid were not new to the train-robbing business. As a matter of fact, they had had good success and had gained sufficient reputation for Cole Dyer to seek them out as he planned the robbery.

That afternoon, the four of them had ridden out to the Black Oak switch eight miles out from the Creek

1

capital, Okmulgee, and got the lay of the country. Dyer gave each man final instructions and pointed out the best places to be when the train hit the switch. It was a kind of rehearsal, the four desperadoes carrying out Dyer's plan. After that, Dyer went home, telling them to stay sober and to meet him at the switch before eleven o'clock that night. Ellis and Russell went back to town for some supplies. Reid and Roots made a camp about two miles up a creek and went to sleep.

Now Reid had cut the lock and stood waiting for the train. Dyer hadn't shown. That bothered Reid. He did not fancy a train robbery run from somewhere else. It was as if Dyer were keeping himself safe and clean of the dirty work. Reid could not see a robber doing that — he could not ask his men to do something he couldn't do and keep their respect long. But times were changing, Reid thought, and outlawing wasn't what it used to be.

In fact, as Reid stood in the full

blast of the November wind, he began to feel colder inside than out. He suspected perfidy from Dyer. There was something wrong about the whole business. That's what Reid thought at first, but some voice inside called his instinct liar. *You're just getting old, Pace,* it said. *Losing your nerve. It ain't no fun anymore 'cause you're scared and cold inside from thinkin' too much about what might go wrong. Once a man starts thinkin' like that, his days on the outlaw train are short. You're listening for the wings, Pace.*

I ain't old, Pace said back to the voice. *I won't be thirty for a couple of weeks. And I never been a coward, never. But after ten years in this business, a man knows some things. If somebody don't kill you, you're likely to kill them, and killing's trouble. This is a dangerous business. Once you know that and keep at it, you're either a brave man or a fool. You ain't no coward.*

For a few minutes, Reid had the voice satisfied. He knew he wasn't a coward. He'd go through with this robbery if a cavalry troop was on the train. The cold inside was something else. Reid didn't have a name for it, just an uncomfortable feeling like he ate too much and needed to walk it off.

When Reid thought about eating, he thought about home. That was funny to Reid. He hadn't been home for five years, and he must have eaten several thousand meals in a hundred places since then. But when he thought of food, he thought of the big white kitchen at home. It was farm food, but it filled a man. Maybe part of the filling came from knowing where the food came from, from the sweat and days of back-busting work of growing it.

Reid started to think about farming again. The voice laughed at him. *Hypocrite*, it said. *The north wind has slid off this hill and picked your pockets for guts. You're desperate, Pace. You gave up farming ten years ago when you snagged onto $6,252 for your part* *robbing the Santa Fe express. Right then you knew thieving beat the hell out of chopping cotton and chasing a mule behind a plow through rocky ground.*

Reid agreed with the voice. "That $6,252 sure done it," he said aloud.

"What say?" Thom Roots said beside him.

"I said I'm standin' here freezin' to damn death for a man I don't trust 'cause of $6,252 I made ten year ago robbin' a damn train. That first robbery put me right out of thinking about honest work," Reid answered his friend.

The Cherokee, Thom Roots, did not try to make sense of what Reid said. "I'm going up the track," he said, and walked away, his carbine draped loosely over his forearm. He walked easily, calm as a hunter out for sport. Reid watched him go stepping along the ties until he crossed the far rail and disappeared into the night and brush.

Reid had ridden with Roots for a

long time. A full-blooded Cherokee, Roots knew the country better than God. Why, God would have to ask Thom for directions. And Thom had sand, too. Bullets flying never bothered him. He hardly ever bent over to dodge them. Said he had medicine. Thom had been on every robbery Reid had lately and hadn't been shot once. Being careful, Reid had been hit four times in the last year.

Reid thought about the way he always seemed to be getting shot. He always had had wound trouble. Maybe that was why he never turned into a big robber, he thought. Two or three good jobs a year was all he needed. Of course, if times were rough, he did more robbing, but two or three jobs a year was usually enough.

Two or three jobs wouldn't suit Dyer, Reid thought. Dyer wanted to be a big robber, pull big jobs and lots of them. That started Reid wondering about Dyer again. Where was he?

Reid pulled out his big gold watch.

He saw the face plainly in the moonlight. The hand just eased past eleven as he watched. The train had left Okmulgee. Five, ten minutes, the men waiting at the switch would hear her and have to make a move. Reid saw Thom light a cigarette back in the brush. He was higher up and farther down the track now. He knew Ellis and Russell were back there somewhere waiting. They were good boys. Local men. Russell lived farther out in the Roost, but he'd be home for breakfast. Ellis was a neighbor of Dyer's.

The thought came again. Where was Dyer? Again, Reid pulled out the watch. The hand had not moved. What kind of *hombre* was this Dyer, anyway? He'd got up the robbery, that's all. He came to Catoosa and sat down at the card table with Roots and Reid. They played a hand or two and pulled out to drink awhile. That's when it happened, one thing leading to another.

Dyer trotted out the plan to rob a train. Just speculating, of course, on how easy it would be. He knew a man he could trust in Dallas who knew when money was shipped out. That was the talk in September.

Later, they met again. The man in Dallas had passed a date to Dyer, and Dyer needed help. His place was about a mile from the Black Oak switch, deep in Robber's Roost. He knew just how to do everything but had to have help in case there were extra guards and to hit the passenger cars. All the men had to do was take the money and scatter until spring. Shoot, Dyer said he and Ellis and Russell might even join the posse. That was smooth thinking. Roots and Reid were not slow-witted either. It was a good plan. What worried Reid was the small and insignificant fact that he alone was an outsider in the nations. Even Roots had grown up and had a homeplace within ten miles of the switch. They'd all just head home and live as usual. Reid would be odd man out when they split up. He'd have to get to

Johny Jim's fast and lay low till spring. Well, Reid thought then, that was his problem. None of them had anything to do with the situation he was in. No need to blame anyone or play crybaby 'cause their chances were better than his of getting clean away.

Was Dyer to be trusted? Reid had thought so until the last hour. He'd checked, or at least Thom Roots had, with Johny Jim. Dyer was a pure crook. He had no song to sing against the others unless he planned to vacation in Detroit prison a few years. He'd boarded at Mrs. Jim's outlaw ranch on several occasions when the Fort Smith marshals smelled a rat and spelled it Cole Dyer.

Johny Jim's word was good as a government bond. She was a white woman, an educated woman once, who lived out on the Canadian with her two Indian children and ran an outlaw ranch. Her Cherokee husband, Porter Jim, had been a smart outlaw who gave the railroads and Judge Parker fits until he was gunned down at a green corn dance two years ago. Johny Jim loved the Cherokee warrior and never looked around for a new man. She made her way boarding outlaws and working the law for them through a Fort Smith lawyer named H. Warren Bean. When Johny Jim spoke for Dyer being an outlaw, that was good credit to his name. Mrs. Jim didn't pull fast deals. If she had, she wouldn't have lasted anytime with the Indians. Indians were mostly honest folks, and they held her in high regard.

Thom Roots' gobble across the night recalled Reid to the moment. The train was coming. Reid's hands gripped the long steel lever. A small voice inside said, *Run. Pull out, boy. This ain't your night.*

But Reid fought it, "Hell," he said aloud. "If we had to, me and Thom could handle this little stick 'em up ourselves. To hell with Cole Dyer." As the light from the engine bounced off the hill at the bend, Pace Reid threw the switch and ran for his sticks. His next task was to dynamite the door on the express car.

When the engineer saw the lights turn on the switch, he pulled down hard on the whistle. The high-pitched sound in the still winter night nearly split Reid's ears. He hoped quickly that the horses were tied good. The whistle signaled the seven men in the express car of trouble. Deputy U.S. Marshal Ruven Blood slammed the heavy bolt down on the sliding door as the railroad detectives quashed cigars and moved into positions around the wooden car.

Before the train had stopped, Reid was outside the car with sticks. "Throw out your hardware, gents, or pay the piper," he called out, expecting the guns to come out. But bullets were the response. It was plain to Reid the occupants of the express car were not amateurs. They fired at anything that moved, and they had the firepower. "Thievin' is just not what it used to be," Reid said to himself. "It's lost its innocence. It ain't lighthearted no more. The railroads and their damned detectives and professional shooters have ruined the whole thing."

2

PACE REID was not a man to cry about what he could not change.

He pressed himself close against the side of the express car, holding a dynamite stick in one hand, the bundle in the other. One of the shooters angled down his rifle through a shooting slit, trying to hit Reid. The bullet kicked dirt near his boot. Just to the side of him, a slug ripped through the wall of the car, sending splinters into Reid's sleeve. "By thunder, you boys are fierce," he said, drawing himself into a smaller space.

Reid had to plant the dynamite in the door and light it. Then get away *pronto, muy* damn fast. From the number of guns shooting, there were six or seven men inside. Too many. Chances were two or three men in the car would be killed. Robbing and killing were not the same to Reid. He'd use his head for better things than stretching rope.

The situation was serious, too heated up. He'd have to cool it down. If bluff didn't work, a man had to use his brain. He looked up at the door and jumped, pulling the locking bolt through on the outside with a cold, rasping sound. "You're my prisoners," he said, running alongside the car to the passenger cars. He stuffed dynamite into his coat pockets. "Might as well pluck what daisies I may while you think about my offer." He slipped up the metal steps and kicked the door of the lighted passenger car hard.

When Pace Reid stepped into the light, he had a cocked pistol in each hand pointed directly at the people. "Look smart now," he said. "I ain't in a killin' mood. All I want is your valuables and we won't have no trouble."

Reid was a good-sized man with a heavy growth of beard. His gray wool coat had the collar up, and his slouch hat hid his eyes. From the end of a .44 revolver, he looked a formidable man. Pulling a feed sack from his belt, he tossed it at a young man sitting alone at the front of the aisle.

"Carry that round for the contributions, young fella," he said in a quiet, calm voice.

"Not me," the man said. "I'm a clergyman. I'm no crook, and you can do your own dirty deeds."

Before the last words left his lips, Pace Reid brought the barrel of a .44 up under his chin. "I appoint you honorary crook," he said more softly and deadly. "Get to work."

The young preacher took the sack from his chest and started down the left side of the car. He was slow and shaky. Reid wished he'd made a better choice of helper as the preacher politely waited for the passengers to drop their wallets, rings, and watches in the bag. "Boy, you must sure be new at this preachin' business. You all," he said, addressing the passengers, "get your money out and be ready when this boy passes."

A short man in a store suit moved in the right aisle, catching Reid's eye. He cleared his throat preparatory to speaking. "Sir," he said, "my name is Walter Goss. I'm a reporter for the *St. Louis Globe Democrat*." Reid showed no sign of interest or understanding. "Of St. Louis . . . Missouri. I cover Parker's court on important cases like hangings."

While Walter Goss talked, Reid's attention focused on his bowler hat. "Why, then, you are just the man to help me rob this train. Use your hat and hit the aisle."

"No," the reporter said.

Reid stretched his head slightly forward as though he could not hear what Goss had said. "I don't believe I caught what you said."

"I said emphatically no," the St. Louis man said.

Reid leveled a revolver directly at

the man's large nose. "You got a big nose, a big mouth, a big head, and a big hat. Whether you use that hat to relieve the travelin' public of their superfluous wealth or to hold your splattered brain don't matter to me. Either way, it's for damn sure you won't cover my hanging." Reid had him. The journalist quickly removed his bowler and started down the aisle. In fact, the reporter was good help, moving efficiently from passenger to passenger.

The preacher hit a snag halfway down the left aisle. A big thick-bodied man stood up, holding his wallet at arm's length from the young man. For Reid, the boy was just not turning out right. He shot out the lantern beyond the man, sending glass all over a thin, tight-lipped woman and causing some squeaks from the other women on board. "Give him that damned wallet and quit messin' with me."

"This is all I got in the world to feed my woman and these children.

I've worked for it two years in the mines at McAlester. And that ain't light work," the big miner said.

"You're a laboring man?" Reid said.

"A coal miner, that's right."

Reid walked down the aisle, listening to the sounds of his spurs and his boots on the boards. His eyes narrowed. The car was very quiet. Reid stuck one gun in his belt and took the wallet. He tested it in his hand. It was thick and heavy. Behind the miner, he saw the woman staring up at him. The children's big eyes peering over the back of the seat. "You his woman?"

"Yes, I am, sir," she said very softly. She was a plain, neat woman.

Reid handed her the pocketbook. "See he don't drink this up," he said and passed down the aisle behind his apprentices.

When they finished the car, Reid moved them to the next, a sleeping car. The feed sack was already heavy with loot. Again, the preacher and reporter methodically robbed the passengers.

One man in an upper berth moaned and began an argument with the reporter. Reid stepped up, parting the curtain farther with his gun.

"What seems to be the trouble here?" he asked as sweetly as a man working for the line and the passenger's comfort.

"I'm sick," the man in his nightshirt said.

"Doc Six-gun here prescribes you hand over your valuables and get some rest," Reid said straightly.

"I'm too sick. You can't rob a poor sick man," the man said.

"Maybe not, but I never pass a rich sick man." Reid pulled the stubby man out of the berth roughly and dropped him on the floor. The man began throwing up as Reid stepped over him and cleaned out the valuables from beneath his pillow. "Shoot, this watch is just junk," Reid said, turning it and dropping it into the sack. "I hate a cheap watch. Says a lot about a man's character."

Reid had been so intent on his work in the first car he had not noticed he was still alone. Before, however, Reid and his recruits finished the second, he was worried. It seemed that men robbing a train together ought to be working together. Still, Roots, Ellis, and Russell had not shown up. The conductor, too, was missing. The vague, earlier premonition of trouble grew in Reid's mind.

He dismissed his assistants. "Thank you, boys," he said. "You go back and sit down. Get the folks away from the windows 'cause the lead's going to fly pretty quick."

Reid headed back toward the express car. The other robbers, he figured, were still back there. After all, the real money on a train didn't ride with the passengers. And real money was what they had come for.

Reid moved silently down the left side of the train in the shadow cast by the moonlight. He carried the feed sack, now heavy with the passengers' loot. Everything was quiet in the winter night. Reid whooped a signal, and Thom Roots gobbled somewhere near, but on the other side of the train. They fired a couple of rounds to show they were serious and not to be mixed with, but their fire did not draw a return from the guards.

Reid kept low and streaked toward the express-car door. It was too late when he noticed the door stood wide open. The moon shadows had fooled him, and he knew he was in real trouble. "Damn me for a fool," he said, ducking under the sill of the car. But he was late. Ruven Blood stepped into the opening and fired down at him. Reid saw the deputy's gun flash above him. Blood hit him with one shot. The bullet ripped down into his back, down through his vitals, and out across the back of his thigh.

He had no sensation of pain, just an awareness that something had moved through him. Reid fired back, but being upset, missed his shot at Blood by a

21

foot. "Shoot!" he said. Reid fell heavily on his left shoulder into the rocks and cinders under the train. Lying in the dark, he could hear the railroad men hollering to each other and shooting as they tried to get straight.

"Where in hell is everybody?" Reid said aloud. "I never contracted to rob this whole train by myself." He lay on his shoulder and side, looking out from under the train at the brush and hills.

"Back that way," a guard's voice yelled to the others, and Reid saw a pair of legs drop from the car and streak past toward the front of the train. Reid fired into the floor of the car above him. "Stay there, you bastards," he said to himself. Then Reid whistled, signaling Roots he needed help. He looked again at the far hillside, trying to see the Indian. But in a minute, Roots slid in beside him from the side with the open door.

"What you doin' over there?" he asked.

"I crossed up by the engine to get

'em shooting' and huntin' up that away. There must be five shooters up there," Roots said. "Where are you hit?"

"Through the back and guts," Reid said. "You have to cover me while I crawl out to the horses so that bunch can't come out and get me."

Roots nodded, and Reid began to crawl, finally getting to his feet enough to stagger-run toward the waiting horses. Suddenly, Roots was there beside him, helping him run. "By God, those horses better be there," Reid said. "I never knew a man could run shot this bad. Whew!"

The Cherokee and his wounded friend ducked back into a little gully that ran into the ridge. There sat Ellis and Russell, waiting with the horses. "Where in hell have you two no-good bastards been all night?" Reid demanded.

"Right here holding the horses," Russell said.

Reid swore. "Takes two idiots to

hold four horses. Shoot! Well, get down, dammit, and help me get on my damned horse." Russell slipped off his horse and began helping Thom Roots lift Reid into the saddle. "By damn, get my foot in the stirrup, you ignorant idiot," Reid said, struggling. Reid slumped forward over the horse, spent with pain and struggle.

"I'll carry your sack for you," Ellis said, reaching for Reid's robbery loot.

Reid went hard and cold. He drew his pistol. "Why, you sorry excuse for a friend and robber, you greedy no-account nothing, you're dead."

Thom Roots fought his horse and pushed Reid's gun down. "Don't do it, Pace. He ain't worth it. He ain't the one to hang for."

"Well, he's damn close," Reid said. "Damn close."

"Let's git," said Ellis, and the robbers streaked down the track and into the dark shadows of the hills. They rode silently and swiftly, heading for the creek and road where they would split apart, leaving the marshals no trail.

"Who shot you?" Ellis asked.

"Ruven Blood. I heard he was ridin' the trains through Robber's Roost. Well, that's the truth of it." He grunted at the pain. "Shoot!" They rode on, each hoofbeat pounding the saddle into Reid's burning body. "Hey, boys, I got to stop a minute. I'm shot through the gut."

"That can't be," Ellis said. "You'd be dead before this, Pace."

"Dammit, Ellis, I know where I'm hit. I'm stupid, but I ain't a plum idiot," Reid said. "Get me down."

The riders reined up, Roots and Ellis caught Reid as he slipped out of the saddle. "Man, you're heavy. Try to hold some of your weight," Ellis said.

"Sorry for the inconvenience," Reid said softly. "Let me catch this tree here and rest a minute."

"You can't rest long, Reid," Thom Roots said. "We got to ride hard out of here before they get to Dyer's place and pick up some horses."

"You think he'd give 'em horses to ride us down?" Ellis asked.

"How'd it look if he didn't?" Roots said. "Remember how he planned for us to ride with the posse come daylight?"

"Shoot!" Reid said. "I'm on fire. Hell, help me up again. That damn Dyer ain't goin to catch me!"

They rode on then, four men across the moonlit fields and hills. Reid gripped the saddle horn and gritted his teeth against the searing pain. He moaned out loud when the horse pounded down into a gully on both front feet, driving the leather-wrapped horn into him. Then Reid was quiet, concentrating on staying in the saddle. He held tightly on, so intent on the simple act that all sound disappeared from around him and all movement became labored and slow. He heard only the hard breathing of the horse, the blood pumping in his ears. *So this is dying*, he thought. In a little while, he began to lean a little, and soon he felt himself drawn irresistibly by great weights toward the ground. "Hold on," Thom Roots said, catching his arm and pushing him back into the seat.

"I've got to get off, Thom. Got to have water," Reid whispered hoarsely.

Roots and the others pulled up. Only Roots got down, and Reid fell into his arms. "Easy, easy," said the Indian. "Sit here, Pace. Water isn't far ahead now." Thom Roots struck a match and held it over the wound. "It's bad, Pace."

"Hell, I know that," Reid said. "This is it. I ain't going a step further."

"We haven't made more than three miles," Ellis said.

"That's a damn sorry distance," said Reid. "But it's all my system will do. I got to lie down."

"He's right," Roots said. "Ellis, you and Russell get him up under that shale shelf." Roots had already begun to unsaddle his own horse as the others carried Reid up toward the outcropping. He pulled off his saddle blanket and the ones from Reid's horse and saddle roll and followed the others. He laid one under the cliff and spread it out. They put Reid down on it. Roots covered him with the other heavy blanket and bedroll.

"You boys been pretty square," Reid said, opening the sack of robbery loot. "Take this for your trouble." He gave each man fifteen dollars and a watch. "You come on back when it's favorable and bury me. Just put a board with my name on it. Get word to my brother in Madison County, Arkansas, I've crossed the Great Divide. Thom, see he gets my horse and the cash money. Don't tell him it's stole or he won't take it. And Thom, ask him to take care of the horse long as it lives. Good-by, then."

The three outlaws stood looking down at their friend. His face was grim and set, drained of all color even in the moonlight. But he hung on tenaciously to the code that hard riding men followed. He did his job, carried his load, and played fair with his friends. He wasn't crying even now about getting a bad hand.

"Good-by," Thom Roots said. "Maybe you won't cross, Pace." They turned then and left Pace Reid to die with his head pillowed on the sack of stolen things.

"He was a right good ole fella," Ellis said. "I wish I'd known him better."

"He ain't dead yet," Roots said as he resaddled his horse and Reid's. "He ain't dead yet by a long shot."

3

"*TODAY you shall be with me in paradise*," Jesus said.

"I don't mean no disrespect, Lord," Pace Reid mumbled in his delirium. "But if it's all the same, I'd like to stay here awhile. There's some things I ain't settled on yet."

"By the grace of God," Pood Ellis said. "He's still alive."

Thom Roots pulled back the horse blanket from Reid's head. "You alive, Pace?" he asked softly.

"Seems to be unless angels look like Indians," Reid said blinking and rubbing his eyes with his fingers. "Thom, I'm thirsty." The blood loss had parched Pace Reid. He was weak and barely able to lift his hand. But he was alive — a lot more than he expected to be when he lay down under the shale outcropping. Thom Roots smiled and went down the hill toward the river for water.

Reid's deep-set eyes followed him, then returned to the other men. Ellis was leaning on his long-bladed shovel. "Well, it looks like you are men of your word," Reid said. "You come right on back to bury me tonight." Somehow that pleased Reid. The return of his outlaw friends for the ugly task of burial substantiated his sense of order and his sense of place among the band of thieves. "What's been happening today?" he asked drowsily, still fighting the grogginess.

"They got up a posse early this morning. Been hunting up to the north of here. Naturally, they ain't found much 'cept that camp you and Roots made yesterday. They're lookin' for four men, they say. Ruven Blood spotted me and Russell's tracks in there right off and made the story of us getting supplies in. He's a right-smart peckerwood."

"You riding with the posse?"

"Yah. Me and Dyer was recruited early this morning. They went over to Dyer's just like he figured. But he only had two saddle horses beside his own, so they come on over to my place for a couple more and got me up to ride with 'em. Two of the shooters went on through with the train. So there's just five a'trackin' us. But not one of 'em's much punkin' in this country."

"What Dyer say about not showin' up last night?" asked Reid.

"Oh, he didn't say nothin' yet," Pood Ellis said, and spat into the brush. "Reckon I'll go on down and see to the horses. Seein' ya, Pace."

"Well, I'm livin' to ask him a thing or two," Pace Reid said grimly. "He let us down."

"Here, Pace," Roots said. "Drink." He offered Reid his hat. Water dripped onto him as he drank greedily. Roots pulled the hat away, making Reid slow down.

"That's a spot-hitter," Reid said. "I'm mighty glad you boys came on back." Roots gave him the hat again.

"You hurt, Pace?" the Indian asked.

"Some," Reid said. "Mostly, she just burns and smokes inside like a pasture fire. My leg's numb, too. Worst thing, I keep drifting off and seeing terrible things that scare the hell out of me."

"You ain't never been scared," Roots said softly.

"You know that ain't so," Reid said. "I just act like I ain't so I don't burden folks. Most of my life I been a scared man spittin' in the face of fear. Thing is, I don't know why I come scared or stayed scared so long. Looks like a man would overcome it after a while."

"Some things a man just wears, Pace, like the color of his skin or where he comes from. Some wears it well; some don't. You wear your fear well, friend," Thom Roots said as he squatted by Reid.

"What you reckon I'm scared of, Thom?" Reid suddenly wondered.

Russell shuffled in the rocks. "We best get out of here," he called to

Thom. "I got a long ride out to my place yet and won't make it by light if we hang on here."

"We'll bring you some food and water tomorrow night," Roots said, standing up. "Try to last it out, Pace. We'll be back to help you. Do you want anything?"

"Tobacco," Reid said. "I run out of tobacco."

They went away again, Reid's friends, leaving him alone on the bed of dry leaves beneath the slate shelf. Reid watched them disappear into the darkness, heard the sound of the horse's hoofs on the frozen ground grow softer and softer until there was nothing left but empty winter night. Then Reid rolled on his side with his back to the night and the world.

What else can you expect? he thought to himself. *You've ridden a long road to this night, Pace. And it's a long road with no turning.*

"Shoot!" Reid said aloud. "Ever' time some poor stove-up old bird gets up against it, he starts figuring repentance. I'm the same man I was. If I could, I'd be drinking and playing cards right now and not considering changing my ways. Shoot!"

But Reid could not turn off the disturbing thought that change was coming. In the cold night, that change seemed black and sinister, a threat to the robber's sense of himself. He was trapped with the thought that had ridden beside him for months. Alone on the mountain, he could not escape it. The old settlers sometimes saw sickness as a providence — fate stopping a man, simplifying things so he could see, had to see clearly. At the moment, Reid saw pretty straight in the eye where he was and where he was headed. He squirmed away, slapping at the numb leg. Things were not getting any better on the road he was on.

"Holler Jesus, you snake! Get forgive like a old whore. You can sing hymns every Sunday and testify how you repented your sins when you couldn't sin no more, like old man Luther Henry. Every revival. 'Sweet Pace Reid got Jesus'. I can hear it now. Shoot!" Reid said softly, and pulled the blanket higher on the back of his neck. "You'd think a man could have peace when he's alone in the middle of nowhere. I ain't gettin' religion. I ain't. That's final. I'm a lot of things, but I ain't a hypocrite yet. When I done bad, I always knowed it and said so. I made my choice and I'll stick by 'er."

Reid listened to his breathing as the sound touched the stone wall and came back to him. Breathing had an easy, restful sound, and he did not hurt at all. He forgot the numbness in his leg. A drizzle started outside. He heard the first soft pop of water drops hitting the rock ledge, but the shelf hung out far enough that the cold rain did not touch him. His back made a wall against the cold and the world. Under the shelf, there was only the foot between him and the wall filled by the sound of his breathing. His world was a few inches wide, and it was enough. Reid drifted off.

★ ★ ★

When he awoke, it was the next night. Reid had lost the day, dropping off in darkness and awakening in darkness. He lay very still. He tried to decide how long he had slept. Reid felt groggy and weak. His stomach rumbled from want of food. He pressed his fingers against it to stop the pain and noise. Outside, the faintest of noises, a bare jingle of a spur rowel against its shank, caught his attention. Reid stopped breathing as the faint noise came nearer. His hand slid down toward his revolver.

The boots stopped before the shale shelf. Reid could not see the face until Thom Roots dropped down on his knees. "Pace, are you awake?" Thom reached for Reid's shoulder.

"When did you start wearin' spurs, you damn Indian?" Reid growled. "You near scared me to death!"

"I switched horses today. Spurs came with him."

"Shoot," Reid said. "I could have killed you on account of those damn spurs. What kind of plug did you trade for? Your horse was just fine."

"It's a good steady horse," Roots said. "You hungry?"

"Never hungrier, as I remember," Reid said. "What you got for a starvin' man?"

Reid watched Thom Roots slowly open a gunny sack. "Ain't no way we can have a fire, Pace," he said apologetically. "You could sure use some hot food."

"I could use any food," Reid said. "What you got, Thom?"

Roots brought out a quart jar of buttermilk and some *sofkee*, an Indian food that Reid liked. There was a can of peaches and tobacco fixings, too. As Reid quickly drank the buttermilk down, Roots drove his knife into the top of the peach can and cut around it for his friend. Reid ate the feast with

the relish of a two-day fast. As Thom
Roots waited for him to finish, he laid
out soap, a small pan, a canteen, and
dressing for Reid's wounds. He worked
with Reid most of the night, tending the
injuries. When he finished, he wrapped
Reid in a new wool flannel blanket
and fed him again. Then they smoked
quietly in the cold night, looking at
the stars.

"What's Blood like, Thom?" Reid
asked quietly.

The Cherokee thought a minute.
"He's solid. He'll stay. No, he won't
quit unless he's called off by Judge
Parker. And even then, he'll have an
eye out for this case. There's more to it
than there seems with him, more than
money. We robbed his train, not the
railroad's."

"Proud, is he?" said Reid.

"Not so much proud as maybe
sincere. He don't take his job light
like some do. Some of the posse men
was laughin' about splittin' the lot with
the robbers. Blood didn't say nothin'.

He just walked away. Every man of 'em felt smaller for their joke."

"I don't know why they don't just go on home. As far as I'm concerned, it was just an attempted robbery."

"You're wrong, Pace. Somebody got fifty thousand dollars."

Reid sat up. "Fifty thousand! Oh, hell. They won't quit now." He lay back thinking. "I believe they're making that up. There was just supposed to be twenty-five thousand to start with."

"Then where is it now? Right now." Roots said. "Are your saddlebags full? Are mine? I never said we got it. I said *somebody* got it."

"Who? Who got it?" Reid said. "Somebody who knew it was there. That was us and the train crew. I kept wondering where the conductor was while I was up front. Thom, I locked that car from the outside before I went to the passengers. When I came back, it was wide open, and the deputies were waiting for me. Your shootin' drew 'em away. Then we had to get to the horses

40

fast. In that mess, somebody slipped in and got the money. Maybe somebody just tossed it out and came back later, knowing the robbers would take all the heat. Shoot!"

Pood Ellis joined Reid and Roots, dropping down comfortably on his heels. He crossed his arms over his plaid coat and sat back against the boulder to chew quietly. The cold wind whipped his collar and hat brim. He pulled the hat down tighter.

"Getting so tight you got to keep a guard out?" Reid asked Ellis as he sat down.

Ellis spit meditatively, taking his time to work the remaining tobacco into a satisfactory position. "They ain't smart, but they're close by. Never know when someone might stumble on the horses down there. Be suspicious, wouldn't it?"

"Hey." Russell's hoarse whisper came across the moonlit darkness from the deep shadow near the path. "Hey, the marshals are out. Let's git."

Ellis stood up slowly, dusting leaf fragments from his jeans. "What say, Thom, we git."

"Go on, Thom," Pace Reid said as his friend hesitated. "I'm going to make it sure enough."

Roots considered the pale, whisker-covered face of his outlaw companion. "We won't be back," the Indian said.

"I know that, and I wish you good luck out of here. Ain't a better friend than you nowhere. All of you took plenty of chances standin' by me this long," Reid said.

"If you want to go on in and get you a doc and a warm place, we can tell 'em where to find you," Ellis threw out.

"No," Reid said quickly as the cold fear that someone else might control his life ran through him. "Damnation, don't do that now."

"You'd most probably be better for it," Ellis continued.

"Ellis, I said no, and by god, no's what I meant." Reid's voice was nearly desperate. "I'll pick my own time, and I sure as hell ain't goin' in 'cause I'm hurt. Thom, he ain't to help me like that," Pace said to the Indian, who squatted on his heels before the shelf of rock.

"It is not ours to tell, Pace. We all got our own roads away from this night. Get to Johny Jim's if you can. She'll be expecting you," the Cherokee said, and started away behind Ellis.

Reid called him back. The Indian bent over him. "Thom, I'll see you get a better horse. You wouldn't have sold him but for me."

"I was tired of him, Pace. I needed a change," Thom Root said.

"Liar," Reid said softly.

"*Shiyu* — be strong," Thom said, and smiled.

"*Shiyu*," Reid answered as Thom went away. "*Shiyu*, you damned old Cherokee renegade." Reid felt lonelier in the night than before. He lay awake until dawn, staring at the wall but not seeing it.

4

PACE REID lay under the shelf, watching the marshals. Five of them remained now that the local posse men had gone home. They searched each foot of the bank slowly on foot. Ruven Blood and another man crossed the river on horseback, and Reid drew back into the shelf. They dismounted and began to walk the bank. They were below Reid, hidden by the hill's steep side.

He listened, wondering if they would find droppings where the horses were tied last night or a cigarette butt or Ellis's spittle. Chewing was a nasty habit. Reid wished Ellis did not chew as he heard the faint sound of the led horses' hoofs on the river rocks. He still saw the three men across the river, walking slowly. He guessed they were keeping alongside the men below

44

him. Once, they all stopped and looked toward his side of the river. They shouted, but the words were lost to him. Reid felt sick, trapped. Then he thought they were laughing. And they went on, stumbling sometimes over the heavy rocks, twisting awkwardly in their boots and spurs like ground birds of prey pursuing an illusive rabbit in the brush.

They went on down the river as Reid lay back listening for any sound on the trail to his den. All thought left him. He only listened. He closed his eyes, and he listened so hard his head throbbed. Every sound echoed in the tiny cave. Above him, a squirrel dropped an acorn in the rocks. He heard it roll all across the face of the shale shelf and fall onto the next ledge. He heard the squirrel's claws on the smooth, soft rock. Reid guessed the squirrel got the nut, for he stopped a minute, then went away home.

After a while, Reid did not hear any sounds of the marshals, but he became aware of sounds he'd never noticed before — small sounds like the grass as the wind ran down through it like a plow. The wind itself took on a form and shape to Reid, its sound becoming water rushing in streams through the rocks. In the woods, he watched the jays working the rich, aromatic humus, hunters in familiar fields. They called out to each other like brothers. White men never called birds or animals or wind brother like the Indians did among themselves. And yet, lying in the ledge cave, Reid felt his first kinship with the world he saw. He began to hunger for more, to know more of this quiet world, to go further and deeper into it and leave men behind — men with loud voices and dirty smells and evil ways.

Just after nightfall, Reid pulled himself from the low cave and dragged out the bloody sack of robbery loot. He stomped on his boots, swaying in his weakness. Using his rifle as a crutch, he crawled and walked away with the cold numbness in his leg and the burning in his gut.

★ ★ ★

"Whoa! Whoa there!" The deep voice woke Reid. He looked around. In his night of crawling and walking, he had made barely two miles before he lay down to rest and fell asleep. He raised his head. Across the winter grass, a black man was trying to catch up a mule. He held out a tin can full of grain. A little throw-together cabin lay across the stubbled field. It's tin roof had rusted a rich red brown under the overhanging oaks in the bare yard. There was smoke from the stovepipe, and a woman with a bright white turban stood on the porch.

"Hey, fella," Reid called to the black man, who looked for the source of his voice. "Over here." Reid struggled to his feet as the man approached, forgetting the mule. "Could your woman fix a man breakfast? I ain't ate in a day or two, and I'd be grateful for anything you got."

The black man reached out for Reid as he staggered. "We gots food to share." He helped Reid back to the house. The woman watched the men coming, but she did not come out to help. "Get this man some breakfast and biscuits, woman," the black man said as he passed her. She did not move. He stopped then, holding Reid, and turned to her. "I say get in here and fix the food."

"He trouble," she said. "White trouble. Ain't no trouble like white trouble."

"He a hungry, hurt man," the black man said. "I ain't never left nothing hurt an' ain't startin' now. You fix that food."

He sat Reid in a chair at the table. It swayed under Reid's weight. Reid felt lightheaded. He fought to stay conscious, forcing himself to see the tiny room and the man and woman. There was a small cookstove, a rickety table, and two unmatched chairs. The iron bed was made up with a faded crazy quilt. Newspapers and scrap wood covered the walls, repeating the same crazy quilt pattern in the room itself. The cup the woman sat before Reid had no handle, but the steam of the hearty coffee rose into his face, nourishing him with the mere smell.

"God bless you," Reid said. "I believe I'll live." As Reid ate the breakfast of ham and eggs and biscuits, the black man sat across the table, his hands folded on the table top. The woman sat on the bed, her elbow propped against the iron bedstead, her head resting in her hand. She seemed weary with a heavy weight. When Reid finished, she took away the plate and began to clean up. "Could I stay in your barn a few days 'til I'm healed up some better?" Reid asked the man.

"You one of the Black Oak robbers?" the black man asked.

"There's lots of trouble comes from

asking what you don't need to know."
Reid looked across at the man. The
woman was behind him now, wiping
a plate on a flour-sack towel, looking
at Reid. "Aw, hell. You been mighty
decent about the food. I'll just go
on, but you ain't to tell I was here.
That'd be trouble for us both." Reid
reached down for the sack and offered
the man money for his breakfast. The
man studied the silver dollars Reid
placed on the table. Reid knew he was
thinking what hard money meant and
where this money came from, thinking
about Reid, the white man.

"You make a poor man out of me,
mister," he said at last, "to take money
for my house and food. We ain't so
poor as that. Take your money and
we keep your secret for you. We won't
know where you go because we won't
be watchin'."

Reid sat still, looking at the floor.
The black man's old hound lay next
to the stove. Reid offered the lank
animal a piece of bread left on the

table. It put its gray muzzle forward tentatively, almost touching the morsel with its nose. Reid could see the small straight hairs around its nose as the lip moved. Then the hound slid back on its haunches and lay down with a resigned mutter.

"Shoot!" Reid said, and picked up the coins and his Winchester. "Damned if everybody don't think he's better'n me. Damned if they ain't probably right." Reid stood up, bracing his fingers against the table top. He made his way to the door and off the porch into the yard.

There was only one place for an outlaw who wanted to stay free: Johny Jim's. He had to get there. Reid hobbled off down the road. The exertion of walking ate up his new strength. In a few hundred yards, he was spent. He went down off the road into the briars, and made a bed under the past summer's blackberry thicket. There he fell asleep.

When Reid sat up after his nap, he

was uneasy. Something was up. His outlaw senses, warned him of danger. He looked up at the road, expecting something before it came. In a few minutes, there appeared six men on horses — the marshals and Cole Dyer. He could not run, could not hide. While Reid hesitated, they came nearer. "Well, boy," he said to himself, "let's face 'er out." He stood up, placing his weight on his good leg and propping the other casually on a rock. For a time, it seemed they did not see him from the road. They came at an easy pace, the slow, rocking canter that covered ground quickly and effortlessly. Then Reid saw Ruven Blood plant his big boots in the stirrups and lean back on the reins. His buckskin stopped in midstride. The other men followed Blood's lead.

Blood stood in his stirrups, looking over the brush and down at Reid. "What are you doing down there?"

"By God, I'm huntin' squirrels. Whose askin'?" Reid threw back like an independent hill farmer bearded on his own land.

"Ruven Blood, United States deputy marshal. Where's the squirrels?" Blood asked, moving his horse forward and sitting comfortably in the saddle. Reid held up his sack of loot. His own blood had stained it and the marshal seemed satisfied.

"Get many?" Cole Dyer asked, grinning at the sack, joking the marshals under their noses.

Reid wanted to shoot Dyer, smarty that he was, playing with Reid's fear and the marshal's ignorance. He stared at Dyer, then looked off, facing the foolhardiness of any move against him. "No," Reid said just loud enough for them to hear. "Wind's too damn high."

Ruven Blood shifted in his saddle and touched the buckskin's side lightly, setting it back into the easy gate. They rode on. Reid leaned back against a tree trunk. Sweat stood on his face. He felt the wind blowing it cold on his neck where the heavy wool collar had been. He looked up at the winter sky through the bare branches. He just rested against the tree for a long time, not thinking. "By thunder, I hope you ain't called on to cook up a mess of them squirrels, Pace," he said at last. The thought moved him into action and he buried the bloodstained sack of robbery loot under a log near the river. Finally, Reid began to walk across the country, carrying only his pain and the Winchester.

By midafternoon, he was in Cole Dyer's pasture. He stood in the woods, studying the frame house and outbuildings. He slowly circled to see the front. He waited and watched. Dyer rode into the yard about two-thirty, alone. "Dyer!" Reid called out to him, showing himself briefly before stepping back into the cover of the woods. Dyer turned the horse and rode toward him.

He grinned down at Reid as he reined up. "Where's your bag of squirrels?"

"Get down off that horse before I shoot you off it. I ain't lookin' up to the likes of you," Reid said through teeth clinched against the anger and the pain.

The smile left Cole Dyer's face as he stepped down. "You're takin' a big chance bein' here," he said.

"I ain't goin' to be here long," Reid said, looking him straight in the eye, watching him like a man watches a snake. "I need a horse."

"I loaned my spare horses to the marshals. Ain't got a horse for you, Reid," Dyer said, kicking a rock with the side of his square-toed boot. He didn't look at Reid but gazed off into space.

"What's that behind you?" Reid asked.

"That's *my* horse," Dyer said as he looked at the horse. "Marshals know my horse and tack. Can't let you ride out on her without gettin' you in trouble, boy."

Reid hammered back the Winchester with his thumb. "You're the one with trouble," he said.

"Boy, you're testy," Dyer said,

studying Reid for the sincerity of his threat. Reid did not move or lower the rifle. "I got an old mule, but I need it to work tomorrow. Got behind with my work here in all the excitement."

"Dyer, I'm ridin' out of here on something. You pick," Reid said softly.

"Mules wander off a lot," said Dyer, thinking. "I can't keep up with the times I chased that damned mule. I could explain the mule being gone."

"Get it," Reid said. Dyer caught up the horse's reins. "Leave her. I'll meet you down the back in the big wash." Reid took the reins and waited for Dyer to enter the barn before he mounted up weakly. In a few minutes, he saw Dyer come out the other side, leading a bony, unsaddled mule. "Shoot! Be like ridin' a saw blade," Reid said, and circled back through the woods to the wash.

"You aimin' to pay me for the mule and bridle?" Dyer asked as Reid slid off the horse.

"You'll get the same pay I got out

of that boxcar if you ain't mighty damn careful," Reid answered.

"I'm goin' to have to buy a mule," Dyer persisted. "And a bridle."

Reid's head ached. The talk was taking too much strength. He took the mule's reins from Dyer and stepped slowly on a stump and threw the numb leg over the bony back. "Shoot!" he said as he settled on the spine. Dyer came around front. "You got the money you're chargin' the marshals for their mounts."

"Hell, they give me paper, and you know now long it takes to get government money," Dyer said, catching the jaw piece. "It's a good mule."

"Dyer, you're a fool for money. I ain't farmin'. I just need transportation. Let go of the bridle 'fore I kill you," Reid said tiredly. Dyer backed away. "I'll see the mule gets back soon as I can. Go on home." Reid watched Dyer leave, then turned the mule toward Johny Jim's homestead.

5

PACE REID lay against the broad neck of the mule. He gripped the Winchester tightly with his right hand and the reins and a hunk of mane with the other. At times, he could not see what was before his eyes as it blurred and swam away. Reid stuck on the mule, partly by necessity, partly in fear. Somehow he kept his direction. There was only one safe place for him. It drew him across the miles and hours to the care of a woman he didn't know.

Reid slid the mule down into the Canadian flats and pulled back hard on the cut plow lines. He looked across the river, up the road leading to Johny Jim's farm. Crossing the field to her house was a dangerous proposition anytime. Reid hesitated, but he had come too far to fear being killed now.

He kicked the mule. "Hah!" he said. "Get in there." The mule shied from the water. Reid fought him back to it. Then the mule bucked and plunged twisting in midair, dumping Reid hard on the rocks. Pain shot through the injured man, lighting the gray winter dusk with bright bursts of light. For a minute, Reid lay flat on his back, unable to move for the pain, waiting for it to subside, waiting to decide how bad he was hurt.

"Shoot!" he said at last. "It's a wonder I don't give up." He raised his head, looking for the Winchester, which had fallen far out on the rocks close to the water's edge. He lay back. "That's a day's ride from here."

"Get up," a low woman's voice commanded. Reid opened his eyes. Standing between him and the Winchester was Johny Jim. Her little boots showed beneath the long riding skirt. There was a bonehandled pistol slung in the holster belt around her hips, and a heavy shawl covered her shoulders and head. She did not approach him but waited, her face in the shadow. He tried to see her eyes.

"Get up," she said again. There was both authority and concern in the voice. "Try, damn you." Reid tried. She watched him. "Move your legs." Reid could not. He tried again and moved the left leg. The right leg was numb and cold, but it moved at last. "Good!" she said "Good." And she came to him and began to help him.

Her body was thin and firm. And she was strong for a woman her size. Together they got Reid onto his good leg. "There're possemen around my place," she said. "But I've got a stand of cotton you can hide in 'til they're gone. Ruven Blood has your scent, so I don't know how long that might be. Right now, I don't want trouble with him or Parker."

"Yes, ma'am. No trouble," Reid said, trying to carry more of his own weight as they walked. "How far's this field, you say?"

"Up the road here just a little way," she said, looking back over her shoulder for Ruven Blood.

Reid kept walking. "Just a little way," he muttered to himself. "A good farmer could make a fine living on this little way."

Mrs. Jim said nothing more but concentrated on the slowly narrowing distance between them and the unpicked field. Reid gripped her shoulder hard, then stumbled. She staggered, but she held him up. "Looks like a good crop of cotton," he said. "You'll make some money this year."

"Looks like," she said as they stopped to rest. She again checked back toward the river and her house while she waited for Reid.

Reid tried to straighten up, but the pain in his side kept him low. He looked out toward the bountiful field, braced himself against the woman and the Winchester, and forced himself erect. "We can go on now," Reid said.

Together the wounded outlaw and the woman walked across the growing darkness to the field of cotton. At last, within the heart of the field, Reid lay down. "Whew," he said. "We did make 'er, didn't we?"

"Indeed we did, Mr. Reid," Johny Jim said.

"How'd you get my name?" Reid asked.

"Thom Roots came through here. He said you were coming. Paid your keep and passage. This afternoon, Ruven Blood showed up at my cabin. I figured you might be close by."

"Blood's at your place?" Reid asked.

"He's just down the road from me. He left a watchman on the trail in. You're lucky the mule threw you," she said.

"Whatever you say, ma'am." Reid moaned as he lay back. "It don't hurt like lucky." Mrs Jim took off her shawl and rolled it for a pillow for Reid.

"They watch me, you know," she said evenly, without emotion. "I'll get back when I can. You'll be safe in here. I'm sorry I could not do better for you." She gave him a big piece of corn bread wrapped in a clean napkin and went away.

"You done plenty, ma'am." Reid said to himself.

★ ★ ★

Reid stayed in the cotton field all the next day. The November sun took away the chill in his bones. The light wind brushed him gently. Toward evening, the sound of men startled Reid. The deputies were making night camp along the river across from Johny Jim's, bringing the full pressure of their presence to bear on the woman. From the camp, they controlled the road in and out of her outlaw haven.

Reid watched the men closely. They unsaddled and hobbled their horses to graze the dry winter grass. Two went off into the rocks, gathering fuel from the driftwood and flotsam, while a third unpacked the victuals and laid them out. Reid could not hear their words but knew all their movements from his own years of trail experience. As night came on, the bacon and coffee smells rose up on the wind, making him hungry and lonesome.

The men talked and laughed while they ate, rattling the tin plates and cups. Reid suddenly realized the great indifference of the railroad trackers. His life, his freedom, even his crime, was nothing to them but a day's work.

After supper, the cook and another went down to the clear river and rinsed the soiled vessels, plunged them beneath the swift current, and made them clean again. In the firelight, a couple of men threw cards on a bedroll. And Ruven Blood cleaned his guns, leaning back against a log with his legs stretched out flat.

Reid knew Blood by his size. He was the biggest man Reid had ever seen except for a Choctaw he'd tried to fight once at Fort Gibson. Blood was a dark man with a thick mustache that dropped down over his lip and the corners of his mouth. The guns looked like toys in his hands. He spread out the parts on the blanket and cleaned and oiled them with the sure hand of a craftsman.

The weapons and the way Blood handled them fascinated Reid even as it sent a chill through him. It was as if he knew Blood would kill him, yet he waited and wanted to see how smoothly his own death would come under those well-oiled meticulous guns that moved so lightly and effortlessly in the big man's hands. Blood made no fancy or showy moves, did not twirl the pistol into the smooth leather holster, but laid it in solid and sure. Then he put the holster down and reached into his pocket for a pipe. He smoked it slow and easy, enjoying it in the crisp night air.

He looked into the fire and talked with the other men. But Blood was different from the hired trackers. Solid, like Thom Roots said. Reid began to think Blood might be an honest man even if he was a lawman.

What did good men talk about around the fire after a square meal? Reid did not know. He remembered vaguely when he was a boy how his father and uncles had talked around a hunter's fire as they listened to the dogs' baying across the night. Their talk was of the war, lost friends, and hard times. For those men, unhappy men, the good times were all passed. Their lives were controlled by forces beyond them. The remembrance made Reid uncomfortable. He twisted his leg, confirming the numbness within it again.

He was just a kid when he started to prowl about, looking for more than defeat and resignation. Just a gangly, rawboned kid when he stumbled into a big horse pistol pointed right at his unwhiskered face. "Hold 'er right there, whup," the coarse voice behind it said. "You flushin' quail for the law?"

"Hell, no mister," he'd managed to say, his eyes still on the heavy old gun. "I just came out here for a smoke, and then I was aimin' to fetch home the cows 'fore my pap got too sore."

The gun came down, and the boy heard the hammer release. "Be goin' on now," the man'd said, and Reid had run off after the balky old cows, forgetting his smoke and suddenly excited and curious about this intruder in his familiar woods.

Reid did not mention his discovery at home, not to his brother, Matt, and certainly not to his pa. His father was not a frivolous man. Speculation and idle talk did not interest him. In bed that night, Pace had thought about the man in the woods, and he knew he was an outlaw. The idea that a man like that would find a resting place so near his quiet home intrigued him. He had gotten up and put on his too-short britches over his ragged nightshirt and sneaked out the window across the lean-to shed roof, beside the barn, and down the meadow path until he saw the tiniest flicker of a fire. He'd dropped down then, moving with the stealth of an Indian until he could see the men in the circle of light, shadows playing over their faces.

And there was his pa, and he was not the same tired old hill farmer. He was laughing and swapping tales with the two outlaws. And the boy had crawled forward on his belly, straining to hear the words. They had talked late on the war and the adventure of it, the bold or foolish raids. The pure pleasure of danger animated the old comrades in arms.

Pace had seen his father that night as a man and not a broken drudge dragging life out of the recalcitrant hill land. For a few days, there was spit in his pa's eyes and spark in his movements. And then they were gone, just like the two old soldier outlaws. And only the burned-out fire showed that the men had been there at all.

For a long time, Pace had returned

to the spot in the little clearing below the spring. Once, from the meadow's edge, he had seen his father here, head down, studying the dead fire. "You shouldn't have quit, pa," the boy said to himself, and gripped his cow prod tighter. "You shouldn't have quit." But the boy and the man had never talked about the outlaws who came and went.

Reid left the farm when he was sixteen. It was easy to leave. He never looked back at his mother and father and brother standing on the porch. He told himself there wasn't room enough there anymore, not with his brother soon to take a wife. An Arkansas farm wasn't big enough for Pace Reid when he turned sixteen. The corn and taters it grew couldn't feed his hunger. He drifted into Fort Smith, taking to the saloon life and bad company. A time or two, he rode shotgun with a freighter to Fort Gibson in the Territory. Even then, Reid was a hand with a gun. He met Thom

Roots in Indian Country. And they ran together, like the blended whiskey they delivered to the big Indians. That was how Reid met Cap Starr.

Cap Starr was man of the lost way, bigger than life and full of all the blow and style the boys craved. He wore his old revolver butt forward high at the waist in the same fine leather holster he'd carried twenty years before the war. His high-topped boots gleamed with the spit and polish of an officer and a *bona fide* gentleman. He always touched his hat to the passing ladies and stepped aside to make room for their wide skirts. He never swore. And he was a badman.

Reid had liked the outlaw fires when he was a young man. Starr was magic when he talked of the war. His eyes danced with the remembered glory of long-faded scenes. There were other men, too, with other tales. They told of the Jameses and the Youngers, of the war and the injustice it brought to them all. The very air crackled with the charge of defiant men and adventure.

"She's not my country anymore," Cap Starr said. He'd been a captain of guerrilla raiders in the war. "I never surrendered, never will. I can't vote, have no say whatsoever, and the billyboys always push around trying to whip me. Their paps couldn't do 'er, and by god, the whelps can't, either."

The war was over fifteen years for most folks when the boy Reid heard Starr's words. He himself had been born during the war, too late to remember any of it or how it came to be. He remembered little of the bitter Reconstruction except a vague dread of some dark, unnamed power beyond the closed door of the log and frame farmhouse. Yet there was shared memory in the old outlaw's words, and there was a grand defiance in his words and style of life. Whupped but undefeated. Beaten but not down. There was hope in the idea for a boy afraid and unsure in a hard world.

By the 1870s, the railroad stood for

all the injustice to the old soldier and to the young men. The iron rails were a burglar's pry bar tearing the Indians and poor from their land. It was plain the railroad was the enemy. Reid rode against it with purpose and pleasure. Cap Starr planned the robbery like a raid. The $6,252 on the Santa Fe job was just a sign of confirmation of Reid's destiny.

As the years passed, the stories swapped around the fires grew more and more into coarse tales of lewd women and two-bit robberies of ignorant Indians and greenhorn travellers. They lost the feel of purpose as new men came and the old men lost the vision. There was not so much shared as the men drifted in and out of the camps, running from the relentless justice of Parker's court. After Starr's death, there was more drinking for Reid, more hunger for oblivion, to avoid the others and the man he had become. Then outlaws did not share common talk of home or family for fear of betrayal, for there was no more honor, no more bond. Only the Dyers were left.

Reid fell asleep in the cotton field wondering where the life changed. He missed Cap Starr.

6

ABOUT midafternoon the next day, the smell of smoke filled Reid's nostrils. He coughed and opened his eyes. Along the river rose a heavy black cloud. The dry cane brakes popped and crackled and went up in consuming fire. Reid laughed aloud. So the marshals were trying to burn him out of the bottom. But before Reid got all the pleasure out of the misguided hunt, he heard people yelling out on the road beyond the cotton field and raised up on his elbow. A group of farmers were mad as hell and yelling at a marshal keeping them back from the river. If the wind shifted, their bottomland cotton would go up — a year's work gone in smoke. Reid lay back. Although Reid had no use for farmers, for some reason he didn't like seeing the law run over the dirt poor men whose life and hope balanced on a few acres of cotton. It was a good crop, too good to lose now at picking time.

The day dragged on heavy on Reid's mind. The deputy marshals were not a joke. The farmers were no joke. Things were just too burdensome for Reid. He'd never been hunted so hard or so long. He still had his freedom. But the way things were piling up, even that was tedious to him.

Maybe it was the simple tediousness that really killed Cap Starr, Reid thought, lying in the cotton field, brushed by the warm sun and light wind. Maybe Starr just got tired of living between the oblivion of drink and the boredom that was relieved only by increasing violence. Starr was Reid's true hero. Reid had loved him like his father, only more. Somehow the old soldier was a man who just drew other men to him. Nothing phased him. He knew what to do. Whatever life threw at him, he threw back, and worse if need be. Starr wasn't a quitter. Reid admired

that. He tenaciously stuck his course
— good or bad. In the beginning, it
was a high course.

* * *

The soldiers had Reid dead cold
on the whiskey wagon. There were
ten full kegs, and he was deep in
the Territory. The law said plainly
that bringing whiskey into the Indian
country meant confiscation, fine, and
prison. Reid knew. He was nineteen
then. He watched the skinny soldier
walk around to the rear of the wagon
and lift the tarp. He heard the hatchet
bust the wooden top, heard the whiskey
running on the ground like horse
urine.

"It's whiskey," the soldier said matter-
of-factly to his sergeant.

The sergeant, standing by Reid's
rifle, said, "Get down, boy. You got
yourself some trouble." He took the
rifle and stepped away, waiting for Reid
to climb down. Reid stood up.

"Let's hang him," a deep voice said behind him. Reid turned quickly. There, in the timber with five rough-looking men, sat Cap Starr. Starr rode tall in the fine leather saddle on the blooded horse. There was an energy about him, the sense that every nerve was alert and about to explode. He was the embodiment of the boy's dream of the dashing cavalry officer even twenty years after the lost war. Every one of the men with him wore some remnant of a Confederate uniform — a cap, pants, belt buckle, spurs.

Reid felt for a moment that he had stepped back in time. The six men rode out of the trees, then down onto the road around the wagon and the soldiers. Two of them threw a rope over a big tree branch. Reid thought about running. He considered the difficulty men on horseback would have catching him in the thick woods, if he got that far. He considered it, but he could not move.

"Fetch up the soldier's horse to put

him on," Cap Starr said. The men with Starr quickly had the horses of the sergeant and the other soldier. "Step off that wagon onto the horse," Starr commanded him. Reid did. The man holding it led him toward the tree with the rope dangling from it. Reid's eyes locked onto the noose. He followed it back and forth as it swung slowly in the air. An Indian-looking boy put the noose over his head roughly, scraping his ear raw in the process. Reid looked then into the steady eyes of his hangman. Thom Roots was not much older than he was, but he had a look that stopped Reid for a minute.

"Shoot!" said Reid. "This is ridiculous."

"Be quiet. You'll think ridiculous if you don't keep shut," said Roots.

"You can't hang that boy for whiskey peddling," the sergeant said loudly as he strode to where Roots and Reid sat under the hanging tree. "This is ridiculous. Who do you think you are, anyway?"

"Captain Alfonse Augustus Starr,

C.S.A., at your service, you niggardly churl," Starr said, riding closer. "Hang him, Thom."

"Hey, this ain't right," Reid shouted.

Thom Roots hit Reid's horse with a thwack and sent the horse flying from under him. Reid felt it go even as he stretched out his feet for the lost stirrups. He stayed in midair for a long moment as the rope went taut. "Use your hands, boy," Roots yelled at him.

Reid suddenly realized his hands were not tied. He caught the tightening noose around his neck. He pushed it away hard as it cut into his hands. He hit on his boots with a hard thud before falling onto the dry dusty ground. "Hot damn!" He swore, struggling to get upright. Reid ripped the rope away and threw it on the ground as if it were a live snake.

"Yeeha," whooped one of the old rebs. Almost instantly, Reid heard the smooth, well-oiled click of six pistols cocked on the two soldiers.

Reid blinked, his anger giving way to confusion.

"Move up against that tree, blue boys," Starr said. "Will you do the honor of securing these two Yankees to the tree with that rope, son?" Reid picked up the rope blindly and began wrapping it around the soldiers and the tree.

"Here, boy, get some hustle on," said Jack Patrick, the Reb who had held the other end of Reid's execution rope. "I wouldn't have dropped you so far if you'd used your hands sooner," He quickly put another line around the soldier's feet. "You can't kick about this." He smiled at the red-faced sergeant. "Sakes, I hope your face don't freeze like that."

"Sorry for the inconvenience," Starr said formally to the sergeant. "You are going to have to live on your pay this month. You won't be splitting any confiscated goods. Ain't that a dreadful shame, gentlemen."

Starr turned his attention to Reid

then. "What's your name, whup?"

"By god, Pacer Reid's my name," said Reid, looking Starr squarely in the face.

Starr smiled. "You say that like you mean it, Reid. You must be a man of the old school. Take that whiskey along now to whoever it belongs to." Starr spun his horse in the sure, extravagant way of a cavalry officer and rode away. "Bring that busted barrel for our trouble," he said as he passed the wagon. "Ain't war hell!" His deep laugh drifted back over his shoulder to Reid. For some reason, Reid smiled, too, as he twisted his head against the stiffness in his neck.

"You hurt any?" asked Thom Roots.

"Nawh," said Reid, walking beside the horse back to his wagon. "I ain't hurt, but I like to messed my pants. This damn hanging ain't light business." Reid climbed up on the rough wagon box.

"Mind if I ride along with you for a spell?" asked the other boy.

"Free country," said Reid.

Thom Roots tied his horse to the wagon and sat down beside him. "That's going to my uncle," he said, gesturing to the whiskey. "He don't always talk English. I'll see you get your pay."

They rode in silence for a long time, Reid shy, the Indian naturally silent. "What in hell was that all about back there?" Reid asked at last.

"It was just a joke."

"Joke, hell," said Reid.

"You're kind of a baby, ain't you?" said Roots.

Reid pulled the team up and turned to Roots with his eyes narrowed into cold blue slits. "You're lookin' to get your rear kicked all over this Territory."

"You might be the one to try it," said Roots. "But I don't figure you're the one who can do it."

Reid wrapped the lines around the brake lever and got down. "Get down," he called to Roots. "I been hung today.

82

I might as well get whupped if you're man enough."

Roots stood up slowly. Reid watched him closely, waiting for the lunge. Roots just stood still on the wagon box without making any sign of what he intended. His eyes never left Reid. "Uncock your fist, boy," he said at last. "I didn't mean nothin' bad. I just meant you ain't knowledgeable about the way things work out here. And it's a fact you ain't."

Reid straightened up. "Why didn't you just say that," he said, returning to the wagon. "I sure ain't in a humorous mood." He got in and sat back down beside Thom Roots.

"That sergeant makes a business catching whiskey runners like you. He's got my uncle's whiskey three different times. He waits for the old man's shipment. He gets to keep half the goods taken. Then he sells it and gets money. He never runs any risk carrying it or selling it. Damn, white men are crooked."

"I guess all Indians is saints," Reid said, turning to Thom Roots.

"Not all of 'em," Roots said thoughtfully. "Cap Starr saved your butt."

"He didn't do much for my neck," Reid said softly.

"Cap's humor's kind of rough," Roots agreed.

"How'd a nice Indian like you come to be with that Starr fella?"

"He and my uncle knew each other from the war," Roots said.

"Ain't you got no other family besides your uncle?" Reid asked suddenly.

"I got a sister."

"Where's your ma and pa?" asked Reid.

"They got killed right after I was born," answered Roots.

"How come they was killed?"

"They were Indians," said Roots.

The boys rode in silence for a while. Reid wasn't sure what to say to Roots about his lost family. "He's sure a blower," Reid finally said.

"Who?"

"Starr."

"Ain't no blow to him," said the Indian. "He'd have hung you if the mood was on him."

"Shoot!" said Reid. "Ain't nobody that mean."

"You're in a different country here," Roots said. "These badmen are real. My uncle once killed an enemy, burned his house, and threw his kids in it. And he ain't too bad. Know that and you might stay alive awhile. You could have worse friends than Cap Starr, too."

"Starr's an outlaw, ain't he?" said Reid.

"That depends on who the law is. He ain't an outlaw amongst us. He's just doing some justice as we see it."

"That's mean talk," said Reid.

"It ain't mean," said Roots. "It's a fact. We got a law over us that ain't ours. The Indian peoples are their own. You Arkansas boys didn't go much for the federal boys running your business after the war."

"You're the first Indian I ever talked

to," Reid said. "But I guess we ain't too different. I don't want nobody's boot on my neck, either. And I'd fight anybody who tried to put it there," Reid said with the deep feeling of the boy who hated the resignation he had seen growing up.

There was a bond then between the boys, a bond beyond their age and aloneness. They were both fighters, both believers in ideals. Together they would test any adversary until they saw whether he was the stuff of men or until he proved he was not.

"Pull in over there at the post office," Thom Roots said, gesturing toward a little log building in the small, rough-built town they were entering.

"You crazy, Thom?" Reid asked. "This is broad daylight, and there's ten people standing around over there."

"You're deep in the Territory," the Indian said. "Ain't no white law here. And the Indians are expecting us. They're our customers."

Reid eased the team to a stop in front

of the building. "Get down, boys," Thom Roots' uncle, Asa, called out cheerfully. "Mail's here," he shouted out. "Mail's come." Asa Roots was a heavy Indian, thick around the middle and solid. He had two fat mailbags in his arms. He flung their contents randomly in the dusty ruts of the street with the ease of a woman feeding hens. "Come pick up your mail." He staggered perceptibly as he climbed back into the stepless doorway for more mail. "Start unloading the freight," he called back to Thom.

Reid looked at Thom. Puzzlement showed across his plain features. His mouth opened as if he were about to speak. "Saves sortin' it," said Thom. "Everybody always looks harder for their own envelopes, anyway."

Reid climbed down after Thom, looking at the bedlam in the street as the Indians rummaged for their government envelopes. "That's a sight," he said.

Roots never looked back as he

began to carry the barrels into the store-post office. "It's good for Asa's business," he said. "If there's money in the envelopes, they'll spend it here."

7

"REID?" Pace Reid heard his name whispered hoarsely. "Reid?" A head appeared in the row beside the outlaw as someone crawled down it. Reid cupped the head with his hand and drew the throat down against the knife blade.

"Who are you?" he demanded, pushing the blade harder against the big artery in the throat.

"Ustus Jim," the man choked out. "Porter Jim's brother."

"By god, man," Reid said, releasing him. "Are you trying to get me caught, with the marshals crawling all around?"

"No," said Ustus Jim. "Johny sent me to move you soon as it's dark. Parker got word to Blood to get you sure. He don't like all the time they're taking. Looks bad with all of 'em on the train, losing all that money."

"They're going to burn anybody's cotton that takes you in. That's Parker's own order. Johny said take you down the Canadian to an old log. It's safer and nobody's fields back up to the river down there, so none of the neighbors'll get burned out."

Reid and Ustus made the log in a slow, labored journey through the winter night. "I was getting to like the cotton field too much, anyway," Reid said. "Too much comfort makes a man soft." Reid struggled into the entrance of a cave made by the spring rains and the log. "I hope nobody's home," he said as he crawled deeper inside.

"Look!" the Indian yelled. Reid's heart stopped hard in his chest as he froze in place.

"What? Where is it?" he said quickly.

"Johny's cotton. They're burning her cotton." Ustus Jim was already running away when Reid got his head and shoulders out of the cave. The night sky was full of flames and smoke. The bottomland field where he'd hidden was already burning. He saw torchmen ride across the Canadian. Three more patches soon burned across the river.

By the time Ustus reached the burning fields, Johny Jim was standing on a rock point, watching the scene below. Around her, the neighbors, farmers whose crops joined hers, were yelling at the marshals, who kept them back from the fire. Some of them had sacks soaked in water to beat out any flame carried on the wind. Smoke lay heavy over everything, adding to the confusion as it shifted and shifted again.

Ustus's eyes watered as he tried to make his way to Johny. Above the smoke that hung in the bottom lands, she seemed unaware of the frantic activity. Her auburn hair was drawn back into a coil on her neck, but wisps of hair blew about her head like the flames leaping through the dry cotton. Her eyes went from field to field around the perimeters, checking the progress of the blaze. She concentrated her whole attention on the consuming flames. Ustus thought suddenly that she looked like a rancher counting and recounting his herd as they were run into the stockyard pens. Johny Jim was making a hard count, boll by boll, as the fire spread through the fields.

Ustus looked about as he struggled up the slope toward Johny. He saw her boy, Deak, catch Johny's arm. The boy was yelling at her. Ustus climbed faster, sensing the violence boiling in the boy against the woman, against the law.

"Stop them, damn you," Deak shouted, shaking Johny. "You started it; stop it." Ustus could almost reach the boy now.

"Let go of me, boy," Johny's low voice commanded. Looking up into the distorted face of her son, she caught the boy's arms and pulled them down. The boy towered over her. He drew back a heavy fist. Johny's eyes never left him. "Go on, hit me," she said as she stepped forward toward him. She stood so close her breath touched the boy's shirt as she spoke. He drew the fist back farther. Johny never flinched. She stood firm, waiting. The boy backed away and slowly lowered the fist. As Johny saw it come down, she turned back to the fire. Her voice was soft and gentle then, caressing almost. "Go home, son. What's lost this night will be restored. Wait and see." Her attention was again on the fire.

Ruven Blood cantered by easily on his big buckskin, going up into the upper fields. The torch he carried left an orange streak against the black sky and smoke. Johny Jim did not turn to see him pass. She stared still at the fields below. Ustus saw the hatred flicker swiftly across her face, just a small downward twitch at the corner of her soft lips. Then she was vacant and calm again, detached from the burning emotion.

She caught up her shawl, drawing it higher about her shoulder. "I've seen enough," she said. "Let's go back to the house." She started away back up the path toward the compound of farm buildings. Her head never turned toward Blood or the field he was torching.

Ustus felt tired. All the long days in the lost fields settled on him as he followed Johny. The shot rang out almost in his ear. Both he and Johny turned to see Deak raising his rifle for a second shot at Ruven Blood in the shifting smoke. Ustus froze in pure horror as the boy focused on killing the marshal. Johny lunged past him, throwing her hands out at the leveled barrel. She caught it, pulling it down. It discharged into the ground through her skirt. She jerked it away from the surprised boy and stepped back from him.

Across the field, Blood reined in, pulling hard against the big horse's neck as he turned. He came fast across the field. The horse breathed heavily and snorted as Blood skidded in, in front of Johny.

"Lady, that little trick's going to get

you put away for a while," Blood said, fighting the horse. "I thought you had more sense." Blood was mad, so heated up the color showed beneath the soot on his face. He threw the torch at Johny's feet and grabbed the rifle away. "What's the matter with you, anyway?"

Johny Jim never moved, never answered the irate lawman. She gently pushed the blowing hair from her face back against her small head. Slowly, Blood cooled down, responding to her, regaining his own control. "You didn't do it, did you?" he said. "That's not your way, is it?" His eyes ran over Ustus and Deak. "The boy's new to trouble. He slipped up."

"I'll be ready for the trip to Fort Smith at sunup, Marshal Blood," Johny said, emphasizing the 'I' ever so slightly. "I won't run. I never have, have I?" She took Deak's arm, wrapping it in her two arms like a lady going to a ball. "I'll be at the house." Johny Jim walked away, taking Deak and Ustus with her. Blood pulled off his hat and slapped it against the thick dust on his leg. Then he reset it with force and rode back toward the burning field.

* * *

With Ustus gone, Reid slumped against the log. A year's worth of cotton gone. Hiding him was mighty expensive for the widow woman and her family. The full white bolls and dry leaves burned quickly. The fields were gone in a little while. The night was darker then, after the flames died. A light rain started. Reid began to shake with the chill. He squeezed back against the log, but it gave sorry protection. The rain came harder, and Reid shook harder. His teeth chattered as the cold rain ran off his hat brim and onto his chest. "Shoot! What the hell good is this?" he said. "Get folks burned out and freeze to death trying not to get caught. Robbery is sure losin' its appeal. Now I'm stealin' from widow women."

Reid never gave much thought to women. If he wanted one, there was usually one around. But he had never thought much of them as people. He wasn't against women, or for that matter, for them. It was more as though they were irrevelant to his life, peripheral beings who had no lasting meaning for him. The sum total of his knowledge of women consisted of two categories — good women and bad women. Bad women spent a man's money and lay around. Good women helped a man. His mother was a good woman.

Reid had not disliked his mother. In fact, he would have killed a man for his mother, because a man revered women and his mother above all other women. But he did not know her very well. She was there in his father's household, cleaning, cooking, occasionally entertaining other good women. They never talked. In his whole life, she never said more than two hundred words to him — always the same words: eat, do your chores, and so on. They shared no intimacy. She never stood up for him or took his part.

He did not understand her work. Women's work seemed particularly unrewarding in the generally unrewarding field of all hard work. Even there, a man might bust his back raising corn or stock in the hope of some money and the independence it brought. But a woman worked daylight to worn out without any hope of cash, to live at the mercy of whatever kind of man she happened to marry. It took a mind far different from Reid's to do that. He could not understand it and dismissed it as he grew older as somehow inferior or subservient by nature. Subserviency sickened Reid, threatened him. He wanted no part of a permanent woman.

He knew Johny Jim was a different kind of woman in some way. She actually talked to him, almost like a man, in genuine conversation, not time-passing chat. She knew useful things, too — patching wounds, fooling the law. Some men said she was better figuring a way around the law than the mouthpiece lawyer Bean she hired in Fort Smith. Reid had seen her and Bean at the House of Lord's saloon back in a corner away from the confusion. She wrote in a little book, explaining something for Bean just like a teacher with a schoolboy. And Bean listened in spite of the fact he was the court-bustin'est lawyer Parker ever met. Before he got up and went away, she tore out the pages and gave them to him.

The barkeeper took her a whiskey then, and she drank it slowly. In Fort Smith, women were not allowed in the bars, but Johny Jim went in saloons just like a man. She never went in the little side room set aside for the drinking girls from the Row. In fact, Johny Jim, they said, had no use at all for the river-front whores. Any man who thought to try her out on that score was apt to get some of his equipment shot off. She was not to be taken lightly by anyone. She held herself high, and so did other folks who knew, not the lawful folks, of course, for Johny Jim was an outlaw. But she was a lady among outlaws, just as H. Warren Bean was an outlaw among gentlemen.

8

REID shivered against the log as he thought. Then he heard footsteps sloshing through the rain, which was beginning to pool. Pressing his back against the log, he reached slowly for the pistol on his hip. He barely breathed as he listened and waited.

"Reid." Johny Jim's voice came softly through the rain. "I've brought you some cover." Reid put down the gun as Mrs. Jim came in sight.

"Ma'am, it ain't a fit night for you to be out," he said slowly. "This rain's bad enough on them that knows they deserve it."

There was a great flap, and a wagon sheet surged around him. "Wrap up in it. It'll keep off the rain," she said, raising her voice over the rain. Reid looked in Johny Jim's face as she leaned over him. Water ran off her hat down onto him. "Get inside the shelter. You'll be safe now. The marshals have about gone. Just a little longer now."

"They burned your cotton," Reid said.

"Yes," she said. "Every boll and stalk."

"I'm sorry, ma'am."

"Uhuh." She nodded, wiping the rain out of her eyes. "Don't worry, Mr. Reid, they'll get my bill," Johny Jim said with a kind of quiet in her voice that made Reid colder. "I've got a horse loose I must catch. Will you be all right?"

"Yes, Mrs. Jim. I ain't gettin' any wetter. And I'm out of the wind. Thank you," Reid said.

Johny Jim looked up at the black sky and down toward the river. "I wish this log were higher up," she said. "If it rains like this all night, you won't be safe here."

"I can't swim," Reid said, looking at

the rushing water.

"You won't have to. We'll move you before that. Hold on, Mr. Reid. We're almost through it. Blood's taking me to Fort Smith in the morning. It's too good a chance to miss. With him gone, you'll have some time."

When she left, Reid pulled the canvas over him and shivered silently, listening to the rain and rushing, rising river.

★ ★ ★

This was bad, Reid thought, like the night Cap Starr died — the night Cap Starr finally lay down and quit breathing. Starr had always said he was a dead man. Reid thought at first it was talk, gallant, defiant talk that spit in the eye of the final enemy. But after a time, Reid saw that Starr courted death. He saw the death hunger growing in the outlaw. Starr changed. He took chances with horses, drink, and the law. His robberies lost the detailed planning, becoming spontaneous, revealing more

103

whim and impatience than cunning.

His death hunger spilled over more and more. One night in a card game with a Yank soldier, Cap Starr killed the boy with the same casual ease Pace combed his hair. He never left his chair at the table to do the deed. It was so simple, if Reid had not been looking for his card, he'd never have known what happened.

"You cheat," Cap Starr said quietly to the soldier, and there was the gun and the sound and the smell of black powder and the soldier going over backward in his chair.

Reid looked at him lying in the floor still sitting in the chair but with his arms out wide. He just looked surprised. Starr stood up, took his winnings, tossed a gold piece on the soldier's bloody chest and walked out into the night.

Reid and Roots had followed him for seven years. They saw his changes but stayed as the others left. The greatest chance Starr took was with the men around him. He began pushing the young men who rode into the Territory looking for bad company. He had contempt for the drifters and ne'er-do-wells who came. He did not take to them like he had to Reid and Roots. They did not admire him or his ragged glory but called him 'old man' and laughed at the ideas of courage and honor. They never understood a man who did not care for money. Starr hated them and himself for being in their company. He pushed them, knowing most of the younger aders had not found their fangs. Some backed down. Some died. Starr was lucky for a while.

Then, one rainy afternoon, there came a boy, Nathan Greene, from Texas. He drove cattle to Kansas, killed the trail boss in an Abilene saloon, and robbed his body before heading for outlaw country across the border. Greene swaggered into a dugout saloon out in the Roost. Reid, Roots, Starr and Jack Patrick, the last of Starr's guerrilla raiders, watched the wet, muddy boy come in out of the rain, cussing. Reid sensed he was trouble but did not worry about him. For an outlaw, any new man was potential trouble. Trouble was part of the trade. A clap of thunder shook the little building, drowning out the boy's profanity.

"That's a helluva cannon," Starr said, raising his head from some reverie. "Get somebody around behind that damn gun and give us some relief up here. By god, I'm sick of the noise." It was an order to some long-vanished subordinate. "Where's Jack?"

"I'm right here, Cap," Jack Patrick said easily, unashamedly, for his drunken lost captain.

In two days of rain, the roads and bridges were all out. The men were stuck. Starr had been drinking steadily all that long, wet day. Starr never got up from the dirty table in the dugout shanty. When one bottle was gone, he ordered another. Reid lost count of the bottles. By noon, Reid had drunk enough. His head hurt, and he was empty for solid food. But he stayed with Starr, eating a plate of red beans and corn bread.

By late afternoon, Starr's natural coordination was gone. His lids were heavy, and he did not seem able to focus his eyes beyond the table. He sat very straight, making every effort at elegant movement and manners. But the cigarette ashes fell just to one side of the plate. And as much whiskey went on his shirt or chin as down his throat. Cap Starr looked tired and sad in his stubble beard in the dim light. Looking at him, Reid felt sad and helpless. Starr was almost gone, nearly used up like good whiskey in a bottle. Reid hated the waste of it, the loss of his friend before his eyes.

Greene threw his wet hat on Starr's table, knocking the bottle to the floor. The crash of the bottle seemed to wake Starr. He slowly raised his head. The boy grinned. "Too bad, pappy!" he said, unhooking the dripping slicker as

Starr watched silently.

"By god, boy," Reid said. "You've busted in here with a lot of brass. Pick up that bottle and say you're sorry."

"I ain't sorry. You aim to make me?" Greene said squaring away at Reid.

Reid looked up the boy's rigid body. "Shoot! Ain't you mean, though," he said. "I've throwed back bigger fish than you when I was hungry. Go on over to the bar and pay for a new bottle and be nice."

"Ain't no nice to me," Greene said. "I'm bad all the way through." Greene pulled back his hand over his holster.

Reid watched the practiced move. He folded his hands together and dropped them down on the chair between his legs as he leaned slowly forward toward the holster. "Boy," he said innocently. "I can see you are fast. But that forward-pitched holster's going to slow you up, make you come back a second or two before you can shoot level. A thing like that can get you killed."

The boy bit on Reid's words, turning

108

his attention briefly to the holster. Reid kicked out at the stiff kneecap. As the boy fell, Reid's own pistol slid easily into his hand. The boy slapped for his side, but the gun had pitched out on the dirt floor. "Don't do that," Reid said, cocking his pistol. "You ain't a bit smart, kid. Just ease up and do what I say, and we'll all pass this night in comfort." Greene hesitated, then moved again toward the gun. Reid stood up. "*I'm* goin' to pass this night in comfort, and you're goin' to pass it dead if you do that again. I don't leave no live snakes in my bedroll." He stepped toward the pistol as Cap Starr came suddenly to his feet, overturning the table against Reid and pushing him aside.

"Reach for it, you — " Starr said, slowly drawing his pistol. But Greene already had his gun. He fired at Starr twice, three times, like a wasp hits and hits again. Starr fell back with the thundering impact. At the same moment, Jack Patrick's shotgun burst the air, throwing Greene against the door.

Reid never got to his feet before he reached Starr. The old rebel stretched full length on the dirt floor, one leg twisted up toward him, his hand still on the holstered pistol grip. Reid sat on his knees, looking at his friend. He reached out and took Starr's head in his hands. "Cap," he said slowly. "Cap? Oh, Cap."

Cap Starr's eyes opened slowly. He wasn't drunk anymore. He was bright and clear, like he used to be. "Get me out of the damn floor," he said. "I ain't dying on the floor."

Jack and Thom helped Reid lift Starr to his feet. Starr was a big man, but the lightness of him struck Reid. All the body weight had wasted away. Only the bones and the clothes remained. "God, he's light," said Thom Roots.

"Bring him in here," the shaking saloonkeeper said, pulling back a blanket from the doorway to a little storeroom. Reid and the others had to duck as they helped Starr toward a narrow bed against the wall. Reid put his hand against the rough logs as he lay Starr down. The walls were wet to his touch, soaked by the days of heavy rain undermining the dugout. Reid's feet were in thick mud. He felt the water at the seams of his worn boots. "Man," he said to the saloonkeeper, "ain't you got a drier place than this?"

"This is fine," Starr said, looking up at the timbers supporting the low roof. "It's like the war. Remember the winter of '63, Jack?"

"Yes, sir, Cap. We was glad for a dugout."

"I should have died in the war, Jack," Starr said. Reid felt sick. The old soldier thought a minute with his men standing about him. "But this is not so bad. It is almost like the war. It feels like that time, doesn't it, Jack?" Jack nodded. "I have my good men about me to ease the going. Drink to me, lads." Starr smiled. "God, I miss the war. What can heaven offer an old soldier?" Starr's eyes drifted into the emptiness beyond Jack Patrick. "We should have stayed soldiers, Jack. But we lost our country. That was our penalty — no country, no army, no cause beyond a man's little desires."

Jack Patrick kneeled beside Starr and unbuttoned the torn, bloodstained vest and shirt. The wounds were ragged and brilliant against the captain's white skin. Reid turned away — not from the wounds or blood but from the nakedness. Seeing Starr's pale, unprotected skin shamed Reid, for it was like seeing all the vulnerability of the man exposed, the vulnerability he'd fought to hide.

"The war was bad, wasn't it, Jack?" Starr said. "Men and horses blown all to hell. Rain and mud in the spring and fall. Freezing to death all winter; burning up in the summer. But — " Starr coughed. Jack Patrick pulled the blanket higher over Starr's chest. Starr caught his hand. "See to the woman."

"Can't you do nothing?" Reid asked from across the room.

Jack shook his head as he put Starr's hand down on the blanket. Reid saw tears shining on the weathered, lined face of Starr's long riding comrade. "It's all done now," he said.

"Shoot," Reid said to himself.

★ ★ ★

Before daylight, Ustus and Johny Jim's son returned for Reid. They carried him up almost to the road above and built a fire. Together they stripped the wet clothes off of him and dried him roughly with sacks.

"Put these dry clothes on," Ustus said as he began drying Reid's old clothes.

Reid pulled on the faded long underwear and worn britches. He noticed the shirt was almost new as he slowly buttoned it. "These your clothes?" he asked.

"Some," the man said. "They come

113

from several others, too."

"Those farmers?"

"Sure," said Ustus.

"Why'd you suppose they'd help me?"

"Why, because you need help," the Indian said. "Fetch some water up here, boy, so the man can shave."

When Reid finished shaving and drank Ustus Jim's thick coffee, he felt almost alive. "How much money you think Mrs. Jim lost last night?"

"Man, I do not know," Ustus said.

"Four fields," Reid said. "That's a bunch. Can she live through the winter?"

"She always gets more money," Ustus said. "Money comes to Johny. But she never keeps it long."

"Can she make it?" Reid asked.

"Johny can make it."

"Easy for you to say," the boy said. "You know what those fields meant to us."

"See if the wagon's comin'," Ustus told the boy.

114

"Wait," Reid said. "What did the cotton mean?"

"It meant some peace, mister. My ma and me was going to just farm like other folks around here and take a rest from outlaws and stolen horses and Parker's hell hounds. That's what burned up last night, mister, a fresh start," Johny Jim's son said.

"What's your name, boy?" asked Reid.

"Deak."

"Deak, I'm sorry for the trouble I caused you," Reid began.

"Oh, forget it!" Deak said. "She can't change. She's going to go on fightin' whatever it is 'til it kills her. You're just the excuse that came along. Now she can just go back to hatin' what she can't change. The war's over. Papa's dead. The Indian's day is over. They got us."

"You think your ma ought to give up?" Reid asked the boy, and waited intently for the answer.

"Mister, she's wastin' today livin' in

the past and holdin' to some old code that's used up a long time ago. It's suckin' us all down like that whirlpool down there. There's just got to be some forgivin' and forgettin' or we're all lost, all of us."

"There's the wagon," Ustus said.

"Where's your ma, Deak?"

"She went in with Ruven Blood for harboring a criminal," Deak Jim said. "But you ain't goin' to jail, mister."

"Neither's she, Deak," Ustus said. "Don't worry about Johny, Mister Reid. She'll be home before you reach the Arkansas." The covered wagon pulled up the rocky grade slowly and stopped. A young couple and a baby waited on the box as Ustus and Deak helped Reid inside. "Don't worry about nothing back here, *Mr. Brown*. You just get well." He handed Reid a large leather bag.

"What's that?" Reid asked.

"A spare shirt and some tobacco and corn bread for your journey," said

Ustus. "Luck to you." Reid nodded and slung the bag around his shoulder. He wondered suddenly whether the Indian's corn bread was for the life journey or death journey ahead.

9

REID looked about the interior of the wagon. It was filled with the meager possessions of the young couple — a bedstead, a pile of quilts and blankets and pillows, a plow, a little seed, and food supplies. There was a good-sized trunk shoved back toward the front, and squeezed in beside it was a boy. Reid squinted harder into the deep shadow of the dim interior. The boy did not move but sat still in the corner like some wild thing. Reid lay back, watching the boy. He was a beautiful creature with hair the color of moonlight and clear blue eyes that never left Reid and yet never acknowledged his presence.

"What's your name?" Reid asked.

The boy did not respond but only sat looking at Reid. "He's called Michael, after the archangel," the man

118

on the wagon seat said.

"Slow, is he?" Reid asked the driver.

"I wouldn't say that," the man said. "He just don't bother with anybody he don't know. I'm James Ridge, Mr. Brown."

Reid rose to a stoop and started toward the slit in the front that concealed the driver and the woman from him. He caught the plow as the wagon hit a rut and swayed beneath him. "I like to see a man as I talk to him." Reid reached for the canvas to lift it aside. "Jesus!" he said suddenly.

As Reid's arm caught the canvas, the boy sprang at him, thrusting the keen blade of a knife against his throat. Reid brought his arm back through, knocking the boy against the cloth. He came quickly back to his feet. Reid saw the cold blue eyes shining so near his own and the sparkling white teeth revealed beneath lips drawn back in a sinister smile. "Gotcha!" the boy said.

"Stop that, Michael. Ain't no time for games," the driver said, turning and pushing aside the boy's knife hand. "He likes to scare folks."

"He's damn sure good at it," Reid said, rubbing his throat. "Do that again, boy, and I'll really slap hell out of you." The boy settled back, fondling the gleaming blade. Reid, too, sat down, determined not to turn his back on the angelic apparition with the black soul of hell.

"Where we headed?" Reid asked as he leaned back, watching Michael.

"I bought a piece of land out near St. Paul, Arkansas. Ain't worth much now, but I reckon I can turn it into something. You can get off any place you've a mind to 'tween here and there. I'd like to stop in Fort Smith and get some things before we go on. How'd you feel about that?"

"I don't feel too good about it," Reid said, feeling a sinking in his heart. "I ain't liked in Fort Smith right now."

"Aw, you'll be just fine. We're just country folks passing through. Ain't nobody wants to trouble country people. Ain't that so, Mary?" the driver asked his wife.

Reid's attention turned to the woman. She was young and thin, little more than a child. She clutched the baby tightly to her breast. While Reid watched her, a tremor ran through her, and her hands tightened on the nursing child.

"Ma'am," Reid said quietly. "You've no need to fear me. I mean you and your baby no harm." The woman made an effort at a nod, but she never spoke or looked back at Reid.

"She don't talk much," the man said. "She's a good woman to a man. The baby's made her nervous, though. She never was like that before. Reckon by the time we got a houseful, she won't be so flighty."

Reid considered the frail woman, with Michael sitting behind her, just inside the canvas cover. "I reckon," he said thoughtfully.

"What's in your poke?" asked the boy.

"Nothing to interest a kid," Reid said.

The wagon made slow progress along the muddy road, and by nightfall both men and beasts were weary from the efforts of travel. They camped above a clear stream. Ridge and the boy tended the stock, leaving Mary to gather wood and make a good camp supper. Reid helped her a little with the wood, but his weakness limited him.

"You look mighty pale, mister," she said to him. "You go on over by the wagon. I can do this."

Reid went. As she built the fire and began the supper, he saw Michael and James Ridge working together, unharnessing, watering and feeding the mules. Ridge did the work as the boy watched or held things. He made no effort to help.

"Seems like for the first time in my life," Reid said to Mary, "I'm just good for watching things. I ain't in 'em, I'm just watching. It gives a man a different point of view." Reid was silent for a while. "That boy, Michael, is he your man's son or what?"

"He's his brother, half brother," she said without looking up. "They share the same pa."

"How old's the boy?"

"He's sixteen," Mary said.

"He sure doesn't look that old," Reid said.

"It's his size; makes people think he's younger than he is."

"Why are you so scared of the kid?" Reid asked.

"I ain't," Mary Ridge said without looking at Reid. She bent over the fire. "I ain't scared."

"I believe you are," said Reid. He watched her working self-consciously with the pans. Mary Ridge was soft, almost pretty in spite of the old clothes and tiredness she wore. "I believe you've reason to be. If you ain't, be warned."

"He's just a boy," the woman said without resolution.

"And the devil was just a snake,"

Reid said. "You ain't much older than him yourself. You're close enough to know he ain't right."

"I got a knife," Mary confided. "My ma give it to me when I went home that time."

"What time was that?" Reid asked.

"When James was gone. That time," she said.

"What did Michael do?"

"He watched me through the window. When I got in bed, he came in and tried to get in, too. But I run to my pa's place. He was away with James. My ma wouldn't let me tell of it. But she give me the knife."

Reid felt himself getting drawn into her worry. He had troubles of his own.

Reid got up. "'Cuse me, Mrs. Ridge. I need to stretch out some and try to build my strength back." He walked slowly down toward the stream through the thick carpet of leaves. Near the water, he found a seat on a boulder and looked down into a shallow, rocky pool. As Reid sat enjoying the evening, a chickadee landed at the stream's edge. The small, tidy gray creature hopped about, drinking, pecking the tiny pebbles, and washing itself in the free running water. Reid smiled at the bird's little regimen. Its lack of fear pleased him, too. There was some hunger in the badman not to be feared. A shot exploded behind Reid, blowing the little bird out of the water into a bloody pile of feathers. Swearing, Reid drew his pistol like lightning and turned to face Michael above him on the hill. The boy seemed unaware of him and came sliding down the bank toward the dead bird. Reid shook as he uncocked the pistol and reholstered it. Killing had been in his hand and heart — a hair's more pressure on the trigger and the boy would have died for the senseless killing.

"Aw, hell," the boy said as he raked at the bird with his rifle. "It messed up too bad to keep."

"You little son of a bitch, that

was a sorry thing to do," Reid said, and started up the hill away from the shattered bird and the shattered peace.

Michael caught up to Reid. "I only like to kill things so I can keep 'em."

"Dead things ain't fit to keep," Reid said.

"I can keep 'em a long time. They don't run away from me," Michael said.

"They don't run to you, either," Reid said. "Why don't you keep 'em in your mind and heart or draw a picture of 'em?"

"If I kill one and bring it to you, would you draw me a picture?" asked Michael, his eyes dancing at the prospect of keeping the prize even longer.

"I wouldn't draw dead things if I could." Reid said. "Shoot!"

"You know anything about birds?"

"I know enough not to kill the ones I don't eat," Reid said.

"What's that mean?" Michael asked,

drawing up like a fist.

Reid stopped in the leaves and fixed the boy with his cold gaze. "It means a man don't hurt or kill for sport. If you kill it, by god, you'd better be hungry enough to eat it. That's what a man knows."

"Shit," the boy hissed out. "That's a bunch of shit." He went on ahead of Reid and disappeared at the crest of the hill. The wounded badman made his way alone back to the fire. He ate his dinner silently with the family of strangers.

"That's a mighty fancy gun you carry," Michael said to Reid as though he and Reid had not fought. "Bet it cost a bunch."

"It works," Reid said.

"If you ain't too scared to use it," the boy said.

"I came damn near killin' you with it while ago," Reid said softly.

James Ridge set his plate down. "What happened?"

"That's between me and the boy. If

he wants it told, he'll do the telling,"
Reid said. "He knows where I stand."

"The boy don't mean no trouble,
Mr. Brown. He ain't easy understood,
but he don't mean no trouble. He's
most misunderstood. It's his way,"
James Ridge said almost frantically.

"I don't think he's misunderstood,"
said Reid, poking at the food on his
plate. "Unless it's by you. Your woman
understands him enough so she's scared
to death what he'll do to her or the baby
when you ain't around. He ain't got a
feeling in his whole body for anything
but what he wants and what he can get
for himself. He don't give a damn about
anything but himself. I seen one or two
like him in my time. He's a killer. The
only thing holding him back for now
is you. Won't be long 'fore you can't
stop him." While Reid spoke, the boy
did not move or take his eyes off the
badman.

"You're a fine one to talk," Ridge
said. "Shot up in a robbery. He's just a
boy. All boys is wild sometimes. Folks

just pick on him, 'cause they don't like him. You don't like him."

"That's about it," Reid said, looking straight at Michael. "I don't like him. And you know he don't know why."

"'Cause I killed a damn bird," the boy said.

"'Cause you destroy without reason."

"I had a reason. I wanted the bird," said the boy.

"What you want ain't tempered by nothing, kid," Reid said. "You ain't got nothing inside tells you go from whoa but whim. I've lived among dangerous men a long time without fear. But seems like there's getting to be more and more of your kind, and that scares me."

"You scared of me?" Michael asked intently.

"No, boy. I ain't scared of you. I'm scared life is tipping your way." Reid put down his plate, walked to the wagon, and took out his blanket roll and Winchester. He spread his bed under the farm wagon and went to sleep, using Ustus Jim's leather pouch as a pillow.

The Ridge family and Reid traveled two days before crossing into Arkansas. Reid spoke little more of his feelings but continued to observe the two brothers. The young one, he knew, was a killer, waiting the taste of first blood. Once tasted, the blood would draw him inexorably toward the Parker's scaffold. The dance of death alone would stop him. Reid knew that. Years on the outlaw trail had taught him the fine shadings of a killer's character. Michael Ridge was bound for the dancing death. The only question was how many lives would be snuffed out before his end.

James Ridge protected the young killer. He did not see the death in his brother. Reid couldn't tell if it were mere blindness or the simple belief that blood kin must be protected and supported regardless of their flaws.

Reid rested near the tailgate of the old wagon, thinking about the Ridge brothers, half brothers. Brothers.

130

Brotherhood was a peculiar institution that men of the same blood and dissimilar temperaments were born into. It was not a relationship of choice, but it bound some men strangling tight.

Reid had a brother — Matt. He was older. They were different, he and Matt. Matt was slower to anger, to speak his mind. He was a steady, patient man who found some fulfilment in the soil that Reid never got, never even saw. They didn't have much in common. Reid always felt his father favored Matt, gave him the easy chores while slapping Reid himself down. It was as though he wanted to break Reid.

The feeling of partiality drove a wedge between the boys. And Reid decided to leave the farm to Matt and the old man for good a long time before. He wondered now if he'd been his own father what he'd have done, how he'd have treated the boys. The difference was so plain between the

Ridge brothers, he wondered if it had been as plain between him and Matt. Had his own father seen the outlaw in the boy Pace Reid?

Most brothers stuck together even if they fought each other. Reid had ridden with several outlaw brothers. They usually had a second sense about each other and made good help if they had any savvy. The last brothers he rode with were named Shannon. Darrel and Leroy. They were petty crooks with a blood lust and stupidity enough to stuff a turkey. Leroy was thick and coarse, but he had the same nature as young Michael. Darrel went along. Reid heard Parker hanged them, but he could not remember why. The wagon jolted Reid, and he felt the wounds inside him again.

"We're stoppin' here for the night," James Ridge said over his shoulder. Reid lifted the back flap, looking at the sky and the country. It was darker than he thought. They had traveled away from the main road down into the bushy country. "You'll be safer out here while Michael and I ride into Fort Smith tomorrow. You might be spotted down near the ferry." Reid nodded but said nothing.

Later, at the supper fire, Michael and James talked of their plans in Fort Smith. They would take the team for riding horses, do their business, and return before sunset. The woman gathered the plates and went away to wash them.

"We'll get you anything you need in town," James Ridge said.

"I don't need anything," said Reid.

"Not even a woman," Michael giggled. "I could sure use me a Fort Smith woman. One of them big whores from the Row."

"We can't bring that back even if you need it." James Ridge smiled as he went inside for his pipe.

"I'll think about you at Miss Laura's. Now don't you mess around with Mary while we're gone," said the boy with a nasty smirk.

"I won't be botherin' her," said Reid.

"We could get you some whiskey," Michael Ridge said. "I bet with your money you could buy real whiskey."

"I quit whiskey," Reid said.

"We could buy you some better clothes," said Michael. "You could give us the money to buy for you. Nobody'd know you if you dressed up in one of them eastern suits. Fifty, seventy-five dollars would buy the whole rig. That ain't nothin' to you and your leather poke. Hell, with a shave and a suit, you could buy a ticket on the train you robbed and ride through to Kansas City." The boy smiled in contemplation of something unseen. "I bet them Kansas City whores is something."

"I'm feelin' kind of poorly," Reid said. "I'll turn on in and look forward to the day of rest while you boys is away. Good night to ya."

10

THE night chilled down into a heavy frost, and Reid shivered awake under the wagon. "Shoot!" he said to himself slapping at the numb leg. "Sleepin' out sure as hell stinks." Reid pulled the thin horse blankets tighter around him.

Reid thought about getting up and going into the woods to build a leaf lean-to. Once, he and Matt built one when they were lost. It was snug, warm. He looked at his watch in the thin light of the coals. He looked at the sky. Only an hour or so before dawn. He could last the hour out without waking the camp. "I hate this damn time of day. Not even the Shannon brothers would be up this time of day," he mumbled to himself. But he remembered the Shannon brothers wouldn't be awake ever again, any time of day. Parker hanged them. Reid tried to remember what he could about the crime Parker hanged them for. His mind was blank.

Then he thought about what whiskey would do for this leg and the cold in his bones. "I quit whiskey," he'd told Michael.

"You quit too soon," he said to himself, rubbing the leg.

"I bet with your money you could buy a real good whiskey," Michael had said at supper.

What money? Reid thought. *After a life of crime, I've got almost twenty-five dollars in hard cash and a stole gold watch.*

"You could give us the money to buy for you." Michael's words came back to Reid. "Nobody'd know you if you dressed up . . . Fifty, seventy-five dollars would buy the whole rig. That ain't nothin' to you and your leather poke. Hell, with a shave and a suit, you could buy a ticket on the train you robbed. Train you robbed . . . "

The last words stuck in Reid's mind. Ustus Jim had come at him about the robbery that night in Johny Jim's cotton field, saying Parker was hot about losing all that money — $50,000. The talk was Reid got it all. Reid knew he did not have it, but James and Michael Ridge did not.

Reid remembered then the Shannon brothers' crime. They'd killed and robbed an invalid man, a war veteran, they were supposed to transport across the nations from his daughter in Kansas to his daughter in Arkansas. But the temptation was too great and the prey too vulnerable to pass up. They had cut the old man's throat and taken $5,000 in cash money along with his team and wagon and gold jewelry. Leroy even stole the man's boots, and the boots got them caught after they'd whored and gambled up the money.

"Shoot!" Reid said. "That damned kid aims to rob and kill me sure enough." He began to think about the conversation at supper. All that whore talk was to throw off the brother about his whereabouts for a few hours. But on the other hand, both of 'em might be in on it. Ridge seemed like a square shooter. But they were brothers, after all. "It's sure as hell on that kid's mind. By god, Dyer, you're running up a mighty big bill with me," Reid said.

He closed his eyes and thought what to do. The thoughts ran through his mind like deer, leaping one way and the next in heavy brush. Forewarned was forearmed, Reid knew as he tried to center the racing thoughts on action. A few days ago, things would have been simple, but now his physical weakness limited the options. "I'll just kill 'em in their sleep," he said. "Bang. Bang. She's settled."

Reid pulled his old pistol from its holster. Moving the hammer back to half cock, he spun the cylinder. The shells were new and dry. He cocked the pistol and held it in his rough hand. Reid studied the loaded, cocked gun lying easy in his hand. It was smooth and sleek, beautiful in its way — a death machine, efficient and cold. He ran his thumb over the polished-wood grip, feeling the texture of wood and steel. There were no notches on Reid's gun. His gun had never killed a man. If he had, he would not have marked the gun.

Reid had seen killers' guns before. There was something sick, too showy, about the lifeless metal and the men who flaunted it. He shot as good, better than most of the killers. But Reid lacked their hunger to kill. He used the gun for bluff, to keep from killing or being killed. Once or twice, Reid had gone to the limit. But his luck had held. Seeming ready had been enough; not many men wanted to kill Reid enough to test his will.

Reid considered the deed of killing the Ridge brothers in their sleep. He would slip out quietly, ease around to the wagon gate. His mind struggled with the justification of killing itself and now murder was in his heart.

Murder. How often had murder grown out of fear, not fact? "Shoot!" Reid said, pulling the trigger and releasing the hammer harmlessly with his thumb. *You ain't killed no one yet, and you've had real cause, not just midnight thoughts call to you,"* Reid thought. *"Wait it out. See what happens come morning. Match the kid then. Kill if you must when the time comes."*

But Reid's tumbling mind was not satisfied. He hated Michael Ridge and punks like him, but he did not want a fight. Reid wanted to get clear, get away from the sickness of the boy that called his own life into question. The boy had a plan — leave and come back to make the surprise killing. Reid thought about the plan, the shallowness, the transparency of it before his own knowledge. Michael was the one to be surprised. By the time he returned, Reid would be gone. Reid didn't have to go far. Out in the woods and brush, only dogs could find him. The advantage was his. He'd see anyone before he was seen. Pick a spot and wait. If he had to kill, he could do it then. All he needed was an hour or two.

At first light, Mary Ridge came out of the wagon and built up the cooking fire. Reid lay in the bedroll, watching from beneath his hat brim. The boy came out next and sat down.

"I'm going to have me a woman," he said. "James give me the money for my birthday, and I still got it — five dollars. He don't have to pay for his, do he?" He grinned a nasty grin, stripping the woman naked with his eyes. "Buying some seems like a waste of money when there's so many women for the takin'. How 'bout I come on back early. I'll give you two dollars."

"You stay away from me," the woman said, but her voice had more fear than conviction in it. "You stay away."

"I could take you, anyway, without payin'," Michael said. "You'd do it for the baby's sake and never open your

141

mouth to James."

Reid kicked the blankets from his legs, diverting Michael's attention from the woman. "What time is it?"

"How in hell would I know? You got the big gold watch!" Michael said sharply. "How much that watch cost, anyway?"

"Plenty," said Reid. "Morning, Mrs. Ridge. That breakfast smells mighty good."

"You payin' for it?" asked Michael.

"I reckon son," Reid said. "Always have paid my way in this life. Johny Jim and your brother worked it out for me."

"How much?"

"That ain't your concern," Reid said, getting up and stretching. "When you pulling out for the big city?"

"Soon as we get breakfast down," James Ridge said, coming around the wagon.

Reid watched the brothers eat silently. James was in high spirit. "Just a few days and we'll be home on our own little place. Mary's pa loaned money enough to buy our needs. By spring, we'll have a crop in the ground big enough to pay him back twice over. Ain't it so, Mary." The girl smiled faintly and nodded. "Michael will be good help. No more trouble. Two of us workin' will make a difference. Then, when my brother's ready to go on his own, I can help him."

Michael Ridge was silent during his brother's speech. He dug the fork into the metal plate and never raised his eyes. "I ain't a farmer," he said. Reid heard his own youthful words in the boy's mouth.

"How'd you know? You ain't tried it yet. Things'll be different in Arkansas."

"I ain't a farmer," Michael said, and tossed his plate at Mary's feet. "Let's get goin', James. I'm tired of waitin' while you talk farmer." Michael and James Ridge mounted the barebacked mules after breakfast and rode out of camp toward the main road to the river crossing into Fort Smith.

Reid sat at the fire warming his leg until they were out of sight. The woman soon took the child and dishes and some clothes and went down to the stream. Reid reached under the wagon, checked the Winchester, and rolled the blankets together quickly. As he turned, he spotted Mary Ridge's split bonnet lying on a fallen log. He took the twenty-five dollars from his pocket and tucked it inside. In moments, he had the blanket roll and leather bag slung over his shoulder and was headed toward the woods. The leg and wounds slowed him down, but he kept moving from one tree to the next, back through the brush toward the rocky ridges. Whatever was up there or on the other side was better than what he left behind.

Reid struggled up the face of the ridge, slipping and falling in the rocks and mud. He slid down on the bad leg, tearing his pants and bloodying the bony knee. "Shoot!" he said, but did not stop. He climbed harder, fleeing his adversaries, using the short time for escape.

How long, he wondered, before Michael got loose from James and started back. An hour to Fort Smith, maybe. A half hour walking around looking at the sights before disappearing into one of the houses on the Row. Then out the back and back across the river to the camp. Two hours, two and a half at most. Reid kept climbing as the sun rose higher. "Damn leg," he said aloud.

He paused to rest, looking back over his distance from the wagon. The ground he covered was pitifully small in comparison to his effort. He could still see the wagon through the bare trees. And from the height of the ridge, he saw the tiny figure of Mary Ridge washing clothes in the cold water of the stream.

Reid rubbed the leg hard, trying to put blood and life into it. He turned back to the climb. Topping the ridge, he looked at the valley, and short hills beyond. There was no cabin, no sign of human habitation. Reid knew then he wasn't running to anybody. The only help he could expect was from the Colt and Winchester and his skill at picking the spot of confrontation.

About halfway up the near ridge, across a narrow, open break, Reid spotted a small black opening partially concealed by thick brush. The cave would give him cover when and if the time to fight came. But with any luck, he could conceal it and wait for the Ridge family to pull out. Michael would lose interest in a little while. Reid knew his kind; when anything, even killing, became work, they cut out.

Reid slid down the far side of the ridge, hurting himself but moving with greater speed than careful descent would allow. He hobbled across the narrow defile and began climbing toward the black spot higher up the hill. He breathed hard, and heavy sweat stood on him even in the cold December air. *Climb*, he said to himself. *Climb!*

Reid reached the opening and cut brush to hide the cave from the other ridge. He sat back, at last safe, drained of strength, and considered his vantage point. From his hole, he could see both the ridge and the valley below as well as the edge of the ridge where it played out into wide valleys beyond. Reid relaxed. "Come at me now, bucko!" he said quietly to himself. "We'll see how you like that work."

Reid shoved the blanket roll behind him, softening the hard, cold rock. As he struggled to get it in place, he knocked the leather bag over, spilling its contents beyond the flap. He picked up the tobacco sack and shoved it deep into the bag. His hand touched something. Reïd pulled out a piece of worn ribbon and held it up. Dangling from the end was a small cross. Reid turned the little piece of cheap metal. His eyes narrowed as he tried to figure whose it was and where

147

it had come from. It had not been there yesterday when he dumped the contents on his bedroll and examined the shirt and tobacco. It was not Reid's cross. Reid had no use for religion, although he never disparaged another man's or woman's faith. He turned the cross in his fingers, looking at the backside. He saw then the childish letters scratched in the metal — *Mary*. Mary Ridge had put the cross in the bag. Mary would be alone when Michael returned.

Reid exhaled the air from his lungs in a heavy sigh. He looked at the bag, at the cross, and out across the hill toward the ridge. He closed his hand over the cross, making a fist around it. He drew out the gold watch and popped open the big white face with the black hands caressing the Roman numerals.

"Don't even think about it, Reid," he said to himself. But Reid could not help thinking about it. He gave himself every reason to forget Mary Ridge. He was safe. A man had to take care of himself. That was the important thing in this world — taking care of your own self. Reid had gotten into too much trouble too many times before worrying about other people. The woman wasn't his lookout. If he'd wanted a woman to take care of, he'd have his own, and she'd damn sure have more meat on her. She had a knife, anyway. Reid knew the great chasm between having a weapon and using it, but his mind groped for a rational way to betray Mary Ridge. But the truest way that surfaced in Reid's mind sickened him inwardly. It was the simple fact he could not get back in time. "You can't make it in time, anyway," he said.

Reid sat holding Mary's cross in one clenched fist and the watch in the other. "She give me her hope," Reid said to himself. "Damn little pitiful woman's hope. It's a long time since anybody give me their hope. Everybody else just give up and said go on kill yourself Reid, to hell with you. Shoot!"

The reasons to stay safe shoved back into Reid's consciousness. Reid rebelled. *I ain't never been safe my whole life,* he thought. *I been hanging by a spider web as long as I can remember. Scared all the time somebody'd break that little thread. By god, I'm just tired of being scared and runnin'. Now I'm even runnin' from a crazy outlaw kid.* "Shoot!" Reid said aloud, and squeezed the little cross 'til it cut into his palm. "You're one too many, kid. Mess with me, boy, and you got trouble like you never seen." Reid almost smiled, thinking of facing down the hateful Michael. "You may just be my mission in life."

Inside, the rational, simple facts of time and space contradicted Reid. He was too late. Too late to help Mary Ridge. Too late to change his own course. "Try, Reid. Try. You can try," he heard himself say. "You ain't ever quit before."

Reid struggled to his feet, destroying the concealment around the cave. He held the Winchester a minute in both hands as he studied the rugged route before him. *You can't make it,* he thought, looking across the heavy terrain.

"The hell I can't," Reid said, surprising himself with his anger. He stepped out into the rocky hillside and threw himself onto the strong leg as he slid toward the bottom. Reid hit his ribs hard on a heavy rock buried deep in the leaves. He grunted. Finally, he was up again. He hopped out into the clearing. "Run, damn you," he said to himself. "Run to judgement." Reid hopped again on the good leg, throwing the numb leg forward with his whole concentration. He covered ground. Again and again, he forced the legs until he was across. His body was wet, and his lungs labored from the effort as he looked up at the first ridge.

Without stopping, he started to climb, throwing the Winchester ahead and using his hands to grapple inches from the earth. He fell hard and slid back away from the gun, away from the ridge's crown. He tried to move again, and his body would not. Only the right hand obeyed him as it reached out toward a hold that seemed to move away from it.

"Help me," Reid said. "Help me." The hand caught, and he drew himself forward again. Reid climbed the hill by stones and inches, cutting his hands and face but struggling harder with each pain. "Go on," he said. "Hurt me. Hurt me, damn you. I'm climbing this hill regardless."

At last, Reid was on the ridge. He could see the wagon's canvas again. But Mary wasn't at the creek anymore. As he looked, a mule lowered its head to drink at the stream. The reins dangled over its neck, tripping it as it moved.

Too late, the voice said. *Stop now, fool.*

"No." Reid shouted. "No." He threw himself down the side of the ridge, bumping the trees and rocks and his wounds. He hit the ground at the bottom on his feet. He heard Mary Ridge scream across the woods. Twice more she screamed as Reid hopped and hobbled through the winter trees. "Help me!" he said, holding the Winchester tighter. He fired twice into the air. The sound cracked through the trees. "Come get me, you stinking coward," he yelled as he tried to run. "Come get my money. Fifty thousand dollars!" Reid laughed. "Take 'er all, boy. She's all yours for the taking."

Then Reid was through the trees into the high grass. He saw the woman fall on the ground beside the wagon. A shot rang out, hitting Reid's shoulder. He went to his knees. Two more shots. The woman crawled away from the wagon into his line of fire. Reid fell and rolled away through the grass. Against a rotted log, he came to his knees and raised the Winchester. The wagon sheet moved, and a gun showed briefly. Reid fired twice in quick succession. Michael

Ridge pitched forward out of the wagon onto the ground. Reid waited. The woman was crying somewhere in the tall grass. Reid swallowed the dryness in his mouth and stood up, using the Winchester as a crutch. He hobbled through the grass toward the crying sound.

"Mary," he called softly. "Mary, are you hurt?"

The frail girl sat up. Reid saw the front of her dress was torn away and that she was trying to hold it together. She shook her head. "My baby. Don't let him have my baby. Get my baby," she said. Reid turned quickly toward the camp and started for the wagon. Michael Ridge lay on the earth. Reid looked at the twisted body. His jaw tightened. Then Reid caught the wagon side and leaned the Winchester against it. He threw himself inside the wagon and moved to the crate where the baby lay. Reid bent closer. His bleeding hand reached out and pulled the cover away. The baby giggled and kicked. A smile flickered on Reid's dirty face. He picked up the child and carried it to the back of the wagon where the wind flipped the canvas opening wider.

"Come down," Michael said as he stood waiting for Reid with the long bare blade of his knife. "I'm gonna gut you like a pig."

Reid stopped, holding the baby still in his arms. He looked at the boy. Blood covered the side of his face and neck, like a preying beast. "You come up here, boy," Reid said. "You'll have to come real close with that knife. So close I can smell the fear in you." The boy's eyes darted from Reid to the Winchester leaning against the wagon, then back to Reid. "Go on try for it and I'll kill you when you reach."

"With what?" Michael said with a smirk.

"With this," Reid said as he carefully shifted the baby to his left hand and drew back his coat from the big Colt with his right.

"You're too hurt to draw fast. I can

beat you," the boy with moonlight hair said.

"Put your money on it, kid. I've had worse spots on my eyeballs than this," Reid said, nodding toward his shoulder.

"You used to be a badman?" the boy asked. "I could ride with you. Help you out 'til you're healed up."

"Damned if I'll ride with the likes of you, boy. I ain't that low yet."

The boy leaped for the rifle against the wagon bed. Reid drew and fired like lightning. The force of the bullet slammed Michael Ridge through the air back against the ground.

Reid jumped down and stood over the boy. The boy's eye's held Reid's as he kicked the knife across the ground. Reid walked to Mary and handed the baby across as she reached for it. Tears ran along her thin cheeks.

"Help me," the boy said. When Reid looked back, James Ridge was standing over his brother. "Kill him. Kill him." The words hissed out of the boy's mouth in an unhuman sound.

Reid saw Ridge draw his gun from the belt of his pants, and his heart was suddenly tired and cold. "I can't help you," Ridge said. "You're my own brother, but I can't help you no more, Michael. You're just bad, like folks always said." He cocked the pistol and fired. The boy's body jerked, then fell still. James Ridge stood looking down at his brother. He looked up finally at Reid with streams of tears running over his tired face. "He's my brother," he said, and dropped the death gun. "You best git, mister. All this shooting's going to bring company. I don't think you'd care to explain your part to the law. This way, I'm just a man defending his family."

"He's wounded," said Mary to her husband.

"It ain't but a scratch," Reid said, spreading the cut in his coat sleeve apart. "Just creased the flesh."

"I'll wash it for you," the woman said.

"He ain't got time, Mary," James Ridge said in a wearily desperate voice.

"Thanks for the thought, ma'am," Reid said as he started back for the woods. He felt funny — empty and full all at once and lightheaded. He caught a tree and rested a minute. Something more should be said or done, some comfort, some completion. Reid turned back to where James and Mary Ridge stood with the baby. Michael was behind them, dead.

"Ridge," Reid said, "you done what was right. Take comfort from the innocent lives you saved, not the evil one you took." Then Pace Reid hobbled off into the Arkansas woods. He looked up through the winter-dead trees and smelled the chilled air.

11

BY nightfall, Reid's stomach was in a knot. He'd covered a good distance. But his instinct told him the killing of Michael Ridge would set Ruven Blood back on his trail. He could not go up to a farmhouse for food or shelter against the biting wind. As he walked, Reid envied Blood his comfort somewhere in the night. He pictured Blood in a big comfortable chair, feet propped against a stove. There was a cup of coffee with aromatic steam rising from the milky brew. Blood smoked his pipe thoughtfully. His gleaming Colt hung conveniently near. The big deputy was not starving. Wherever he really was, his stomach was full, and he was easy inside. After all, Ruven Blood was not coming on his trail. Reid stumbled over a root and cussed profusely — not the root but his own folly.

Down the valley, Reid saw a little pale light. A tree branch covered it as the wind gusted through the grove. Reid fought the limb away and started toward the light. He moved quickly, fearing the light would disappear before he found its source. But the light did not flicker out; it beckoned. In his haste, Reid did not see the hounds coming across the woods. When he heard them, they were already leaping through the air toward him. Reid yelled as the spotted hound sunk his teeth into his thigh. He fought the dogs with the rifle butt, but he was weak and tired. The big hounds came back again and again, one feinting in as the other bit from another side. They ripped Reid's thick coat into shreds. Reid fought to pull the Colt. But once he held it, he hesitated to fire lest the shots bring the dogs' owner or a group of hunters. Reid was desperate. He looked about in a quick scan as the dogs backed away briefly. Looking up, he knew. He jumped for a branch above his head. The dogs came in again. Kicking free of the tenacious hounds, Reid hauled himself into the branches.

"Shoot!" he said, looking down at the dogs standing with their front legs against the trunk. The spotted hounded jumped up, trying to get Reid's boot. Reid pulled his leg in. He tried to slow his heart and breathing as he looked down on the eager beasts. "Sure ain't no country for a man on foot," he said, meditating on the dogs. The red hound jumped high against the tree, trying to throw its upper body over a low limb. "By god, that dog's a climber." Reid climbed higher and braced himself against the trunk and a big branch. The tree was a fit for Reid. He rested comfortably, waiting for the dogs to tire or the hunters to call them in.

Sunlight filtering through the trees into his eyes woke Reid. He looked for the dogs. They were gone. His Winchester lay half buried in the thick leaves. He waited a few minutes more and dropped down. His body was stiff and ached from the cold night in the tree and the fight with the dogs. Reid stretched. A groan escaped him. Dropping to the ground, he picked up the Winchester and his hat. The brim on the hat was ripped. Reid cussed, sticking his fingers into the tear. "Damn, damn, damn," he said.

The little cabin was still there, a few yards down the valley. It was not an illusion of the night before. Reid cocked the Winchester. "By god," he said, "I've had enough of this. I've been shot, froze, bumped over every rough road, and set on by a maniac and dogs. I'm going to get a good horse." He started toward the house.

★ ★ ★

As Reid kicked the door in, he lifted the Winchester and quickly stepped into the room with his broad back to the wall. The room was snug and clean.

The two hounds lay near the fire where a rocking chair moved rhythmically back and forth. The high back hid its occupant, but Reid knew the dogs. They lay on the hearth, heads between their paws, teeth showing beneath their curled lips. But something held them in place. Reid's eyes ran over the room again before he closed the door and lowered the rifle. He moved forward to the fire. The rocking chair never faltered. Reid stepped in front, raising the gun again. The woman looked at Reid, at the gun, as she slowly stroked a yellow cat lying in her lap.

The woman was of an age to be called old, but the label did not quite fit. Her blue eyes were steady and clear. There was good color to her and a quiet power.

"So you've found me," she said softly.

"Lady, I ain't found you 'cause I ain't lookin' for you. I'm lookin' for food and a warm place and a mite of rest."

"There's all that here," she said. One of the dogs snapped at Reid's leg. "Be gentle," the woman said. The dog lay back.

"Put them damn dogs out," Reid commanded, raising the rifle at the woman. The dogs growled and rose up onto their haunches. The woman smiled at Reid. Then she rose easily out of the chair. Reid watched her cross the room. He knew she must be old, but she moved like a panther, sure and steady, on a rocky ledge. She opened the door, calling to the dogs. They frolicked out, biting at each other's hocks.

"Who lives here?" Reid asked as she closed the heavy door.

"Only myself and the critters," she said, coming back toward the fire. She reached out toward Reid's head, and he dodged aside as she took down a plate from the mantel. "You're jumpy, boy," she said, filling it from the bubbling kettle of corn mush. She sat the plate on a small bleached table and brought a spoon and napkin. "Sit and eat," she said. Reid eased into the chair and leaned his rifle against the table's edge. The woman brought him coffee, and he began to eat as she sat back in the rocker.

"Where's your people?" Reid asked with his mouth full. "Old woman like yourself shouldn't be way out here by yourself."

"Why not?" she asked softly.

"Ain't prudent," said Reid. "There's varmints and outlaws and numerous other dangers."

"I'm far more dangerous than any outlaw," she said.

"Shoot!" said Reid. "I could snap you like a twig."

The woman smiled. "Whatever for?"

"For the hell of it," Reid said, struggling with the mush in his mouth. "'Cause I'm mean or desperate or want what you have."

"Silver and gold have I none. But such as I have, I give you freely."

"How 'bout a horse?" Reid asked,

thinking of his next pressing need.

"No horse," she said, stroking the cat.

"See!" Reid said gleefully. "See, I might kill you because you ain't got a horse and I need one." He stuffed a piece of bread into his mouth with one hand and removed his ragged Stetson with the other.

"Be a waste," she said, rocking.

"Be a pleasure most likely," Reid said to himself. Reid ate then without talking. The woman rocked, looking into the fire. The cat stretched its forelegs up against her shoulder, examining the noble face. She stroked its broad back, and it lay down again.

"What you do way out here?" asked Reid.

"I just live, boy. Take care of what comes. What do you do way out here?"

"I'm hunting," Reid said, wiping his mouth.

"That's a lie," the woman said. "Satan is the father of all liars, and thieves, too."

Reid sat back from the table and empty plate. He tossed the napkin at the plate. "Satan, my rear end. Who says I'm a liar or a thief."

"I say it plain. You are a liar and a thief."

"Shoot!" Reid said, getting up. "I killed men for less than that."

"Lie," she said quietly.

"How in hell can you tell that? I might have killed fifty men. Them things don't show any more than lying or stealing."

"They show."

Reid walked over to the door and dropped the sturdy bar across it. One by one, he closed the shutters over the windows. "This place is a regular fort," he said to himself. "I need some rest," he said to the woman. "You got any rope or twine?" She nodded toward a cupboard. Reid found a short length of light rope and tied the woman's hands to the rocker arms. She offered no resistance. Reid felt low. "You just rock," he said gently. "I ain't goin' to hurt nothin'," She smiled at Reid. As he lay back on the bright quilt, the smile bothered him. He saw it as he closed his heavy eyes. "What's your name, lady?" he asked.

"Rhema," she said. Reid dozed off, full and warm and safe after many days. "Rhema Blood," she said softly.

★ ★ ★

Reid heard the heavy sounds in his sleep. For a minute, he was still asleep, listening through dark time and space. He fought through the sleep. Reid tried to remember where he was. The answer eluded him for long seconds. Then his eyes popped open, and he knew. In one gesture, he was up, swinging his feet to the floor. The pistol was in his hand as he faced the pounding at the door.

"Reid," a voice unknown to him called out. "Reid, we know you are in there. Come on out or we'll burn you out."

"Who the hell are you?" Reid asked,

playing for time to clear his still-groggy mind.

"That's for us to know," the voice said.

"You the law?" asked Reid.

Reid heard a deep laugh from beyond the thick door.

"That's right. We're the law. Open up. We want to talk to you about fifty thousand dollars you took off a train."

Reid knew something was wrong. He moved across the room away from the door, away from the bullets that might soon fly. He backed up against the fireplace, where Rhema still sat tied. "What's your name, law?"

"Ruven Blood's my name. Open up," the deep voice said.

"He ain't Ruven Blood," she said. Reid's eyes fell on Rhema and then on the hounds beside her. Reid remembered putting the bad-tempered animals out. But another question demanded his attention.

"How'd you know that?"

"Blood's my son," the woman said.

Reid's stomach felt suddenly empty and queasy. "Shoot!" he said. "You sure?" Rhema Blood nodded. Reid stood still, taking in the thought. "You ain't Blood," he called out to the voice behind the door. "Get off the porch before I come out there and kick you off."

"Hearty talk for a dead man," the voice said. "Throw out the money and we'll leave you in peace."

Reid dropped his head, thinking. "Who says I got any money?"

"Cole Dyer."

"Dyer, my right elbow. That henhouse rooster has crowed once too often. Get off that damn porch." Reid yelled at the door. "You got a shotgun, Mrs. Blood?"

"Untie me, boy. There's wolves at the door," Reid untied Rhema Blood quickly. Rubbing her wrists, she went straight to the wardrobe and opened the door. Reid blinked. Inside were fine pistols and a matched pair of double-barreled shotguns. The shelf was lined with boxes of ammunition. "Get crackin', boy," she said. "There's work to do." Reid started toward the cabinet and fell over the spotted hound.

"Where'd these damn dogs come from?" he said.

"Over there." Mrs. Blood nodded toward the wood box. "That's their door," she said.

"Shoot!" Reid said, and reached for the shotgun she held out. "Close that thing up so we don't get any more company."

"Throw out the money, Reid, or we'll torch you out," the man beyond the door shouted.

"Do 'er, by god," said Reid. "And I'll burn all the money I got in the fireplace. Get off the porch." Reid shoved the shotgun into a shooting port and fired both barrels toward the sound of the voice. Reid heard boots running on the porch boards and the sound of bushes as someone dived into them. "Ha," he said. "Ain't so smart now, are you?" As Reid said the words, bullets slammed into the log cabin like a swarm of bees. Reid flattened out against the wall as the bullets flew.

Rhema Blood slapped the other shotgun into his hand. "There are five of them," she said. "Two out front by the big oak on the left. One by the sycamore yonder and another out back in the boulders. He's got the horses with him. The one you put off the porch moved out in the bushes."

"How'd you know that?" asked Reid in surprise, straining his eyes through the peephole.

"I can hear," Rhema said, pouring coffee on the fire and scattering the wood in the fireplace. "And I been through this before, before you were born most likely."

"Where?" asked Reid.

"The war," she said. "I wish you hadn't called the fire to their attention. In a minute, a couple of those out front are going to figure out covering the chimney will keep you from burning the money and smoke us out of here at the same time. You may get a shot at one of 'em, but the other one will most likely make it."

Reid narrowed his eyes, concentrating on the sliver of scene before him. A runner darted out into the yard. Bullets splattered into the wood around Reid, but he followed the running figure. Reid squeezed the trigger. The man jumped up, grabbing his leg, and plunged into the bush. Out of the corner of his eye, Reid saw a second dart around the porch. He had a coat in his hand. "Shoot!" Reid said.

"Be quiet," Rhema Blood said, looking up at the roof expectantly and listening. Reid waited and listened. Another hail of bullets peppered the cabin, but Rhema's attention remained focused on the roof. She heard the first step, the second, but waited. "Now," she said to herself, and fired Reid's Winchester into the ceiling at the sounds. She levered fresh shells into the chamber and fired like lightning in a neat circle around the outlaw. "Get down from there," she said, speaking to herself. Reid swallowed the dryness in his mouth, watching the old woman expertly handle the gun. They heard something fall or jump into the woodpile near the fireplace.

"The war," he said almost to himself.

"That's right. Of course, our guns weren't as good then," said Rhema Blood. "The Yankees and the guerrillas both had their turn at us. There was considerable bad feeling in those days."

"Hm," said Reid, looking back at the gun port. "Considerable." Reid's eyes scanned the trees and brush. He saw the roof climber limp back into the heavy corner but did not fire. "They can't shoot us out or smoke us out," he said. "But they can starve us."

"Takes too long," Rhema Blood said. "Those fellas are out for quick money. They'll probably rush you." She sat the reloaded shotgun and the Winchester beside Reid. "Use that little repeater 'til

174

they're close. You won't hit anything, but it'll keep 'em off balance. When they're almost on us, fall back and I'll use the shotgun." Reid studied the woman's face. It was calm, almost serene. The bullets slamming against the log house did not arouse either fear or anger in her. Reid took the Winchester.

A figure appeared about fifty feet out in the brush. Reid squinted and leaned forward. "By god, there's somebody else out there," he said.

Rhema Blood shoved him aside slightly to peer through the slot. "Praise the Lord," she said. "It's Ruven."

"Well," said Reid, leaning back to the slot. "That ain't no help to me." Blood made a target of himself near a tree. He yelled out. One of the robbers near the sycamore raised up. Blood nailed him as Reid penned his partner with a few fast rounds. "Whew!" said Reid. "He's stony, ain't he?"

Mrs. Blood leaned over to see her son in action. She picked up a revolver lying on the floor. "It's going to get hot from two ways for those boys out there."

Reid sat back against the log wall as mother and son caught the outlaws in a crossfire. He was caught, too. As soon as Blood got to the house, he was headed for prison. Reid grimaced as his eyes wandered idly over the room. Reid straightened slightly as he saw the wood box. A pen was stuck through the hasp to keep them safe inside. Reid smiled. He reached into the floor and grabbed a pistol. He slid away quietly from Rhema Blood's side. As she fired away at the outlaws, he lifted the lid on the rough wood bin and crawled through to the outside.

A bullet smacked into the log near Reid's cheek. "Shoot!" he said, and lay back, checking his pistol. Reid threw the Winchester toward the boulder pile. The outlaw fired. "Idiot," Reid said, and rolled out of the box and behind the woodpile. He threw a log into the trees. Again, the outlaw fired. Reid ran, not fast but effectively, into the boulder pile. He scrambled up between the rocks, using his strong arms and shoulders to pull himself toward the gunman.

Reid slid his upper body over the rock and pointed the pistol down at the figure. "Freeze," he said softly. The outlaw threw the gun he held at the ground and lifted his hands. He was a kid. "Get back there." Reid gestured as he looked at the scene. On the ground, there were three pistols and a box of shells with the cartridges tumbled out. "You ain't cut out for this work, kid." Reid threw the pistols into the cabin yard as the boy remained fixed against the rock. "Shut your mouth, kid, and wipe your nose." The boy's jaw snapped up, and he ran his rough sleeve against his nose as Reid watched.

"Where's the horses, sprout?" The boy pointed. "Well, get 'em." Reid followed as the boy brought the horses around. Reid considered the outlaws' horses contemptuously. "Ain't one prime horse among you. You all must be rank amateurs or fools," he said, mounting up on the best among the creatures. "Cut the girts." The boy slashed the bands. Reid whooped, scattering the outlaw ponies. He started away, but turned back.

"Who told you I had the money?" Reid asked.

"Cole Dyer," the boy said, and ran.

He rode down behind the fleeing horses into a broken valley. The horses cut across the grassland and fled up into the woods. Reid watched them disappear over the crest. Shooting still came from behind him. He turned his horse, heading back in a wide circle to the front of the cabin, where Ruven Blood was throwing lead. By the time Reid had the cabin in view, Blood was in the yard. All the outlaws had their hands high in the air. Reid smiled as Blood stripped away their belts and remaining weapons. Mrs. Blood had the boy from behind the cabin in tow as she came around the house.

Reid reined his horse hard away from the scene. His eyes searched the brush for Blood's horse. The horse pawed and nickered, and Reid rode close. "Now that's a horse," he said of the big dun. Reid slid off the outlaw horse onto Blood's. He rode away, leading the pony. Reid felt the power and sense of the marshal's horse. He had stay. Everything about the horse was right as Reid tested him over the hilly terrain and creek beds. Even the saddle fit. Reid pulled up. "Whoa," he said and patted the smooth neck. He swung down. "Thanks for the ride, big fella. I'd love to keep you, but you're too well known. Ain't no use makin' Blood any madder." Reid pulled the saddle and bridle off the buckskin and threw them into a gully. "That's a waste," he said as he remounted the stolen outlaw pony and rode away.

12

IT took Reid a week of slow, hard travel to make his way home to the sleepy farm in Madison County. His horse pulled up lame, so he hobbled and hitched a ride or two until he cut across country toward the homestead. When Reid crawled over the rail fence in the meadow pasture, he could see the little white house with smoke rising easy through the frosty air. Matt stood in the yard beside the porch cutting wood. Reid waited, still, taking in the picture before him. There was a wash on the line, and a woman, bundled in a heavy coat, was coming in with a basket of dried things. Five cords of wood were stacked in neat ricks in the yard. Five cords — Reid thought about his pa — enough to last till spring. The remembrance gave him a rich feeling.

Reid started through the stubble

toward the house, and a hound let out a deep bay that caught on the air and drew the other farm dogs into a ferocious symphony. Matt looked up from his work. The woman shielded her eyes from the sun and tried to see. Reid began to walk again as they watched. He saw the woman run in for the gun above the kitchen door, but he kept walking over the heavy ground. She came out with the old shotgun and handed it to Matt. Reid saw the gun in his brother's hands, but his voice would not call out, and he walked harder, leaning on the Winchester. "Don't shoot, Matt," he said, too low to be heard in the wind. "I'm your brother." As Reid hobbled forward, he saw the gun come up to Matt's shoulder. He wanted to call out but could not. Then he saw Matt set the gun down against the woodpile and start out toward him with big distance-killing strides. Pretty soon the other man was running. Beyond him, Reid heard the woman yelling toward the house, and his father came out in his shirt-sleeves and suspenders. Matt caught Reid and hugged him to himself.

"Pace," he said. "Pace, you've come home."

Reid drew back. "I'm a running man, Matt. The law's behind me somewhere."

Matt caught him under the arm. "We'll think on that later, Pace. Let's go on home for now."

Reid's father embraced him. And Reid smelled the lye soap and starch of his shirt and felt the tears on his father's clean-shaven cheeks. "Boy, it's good to see you," he said. "We heard you were killed over in the Indian country during a robbery."

"I damn near was," Reid said shyly.

"We'll fix you," the old farmer said. "If you can make it this far, son, we can sure fix you up."

"Ain't you sick of me, pa?" Reid asked. "Mad 'cause I brought the law and a bad name on you."

"Everybody carries the weight of his own deeds, son. What's between you and the law's your business. What's between you and me is my business."

"Ain't you aimin' to run me off?"

"I can't run you nowhere. This is your home place. You worked here same as Matt," Reid's father said. "Your ma always wanted things that way."

Sitting around the table in the big white kitchen, watching him, the family fed Reid. Afterward, they tended the battered body of the badman. At last, Matt pulled the heavy quilts over his brother. "It's good to be home," Reid said. And Reid slept easy in the clean bed where he had slept as a boy. Pace Reid had come home.

Reid convalesced in the tiny loft room, warmed by the thick quilts and a little iron stove. At first, he slept for whole days, exhausted from his struggle to get home and from his fear. But gradually his attention turned back to the world around him. Lying in bed, he studied the coverlet over him. He recognised material from his mother's dresses and his and Matt's shirts patched into the quilts. There was a whole family history in the little faded scraps of cloth. Following the shape of a patch, he remembered the blue shirt with stripes he'd worn at church the Sunday he tied into Zeke Fields for calling him a liar as they sat in the young men's pew. They'd turned over the pew, dumping the other boys into the laps of some of the elders. Reid remembered how the men pulled them quickly apart and took them outside to cool off.

"He called me liar," Reid said to his father. "Dirty trash liar." Just saying the words made him angry again, and he lunged at Fields.

"Did you lie?" his father asked, and Reid felt beaten. "If you don't want to be called liar, tell no lies." That did not matter to Reid. What mattered to him was a pa who would not stand up for a son who'd been called liar in front of other men. Reid jerked away, defeated. "Wait in the wagon," his pa said.

Reid's ma and Matt came to the wagon in a little while. The family drove home silently with the fried chicken and four-layer cake still in the basket instead of with the feast of food under the cool shade of the grove. And Reid felt worse for having ruined their Sunday dinner on the ground. And he felt angry because he wanted his pa to stand up for him and he wouldn't. And although Reid held that against his pa, at the same time truth became important to him.

The door to the room opened slowly as Pa Reid put his head inside to see if his son still slept. "I'm awake, pa," Pace said. "Come on in."

The elder Reid came across to the bed and drew a cane-bottom chair near to his son. "Pace," he said. "We had our Chris'mas before you came home, but I got a present I been saving for you a long time — almost five years now." He handed Reid an envelope.

Pace looked at his father for a moment before he took it. He ran his forefinger under the sealed flap, resisting the urge to say his pa should not have given him a gift because he didn't deserve it and because he had no present to give in return. Reid drew out the paper and unfolded it. He scanned it quickly, seeing it was a deed and that his name was on it. He could control himself no more.

"Aw, pa, I ain't a farmer," he said.

"The land gives strength to a broken man, son. Like the Book says, 'One generation passeth away, and another generation cometh, but the earth abideth forever,'" his pa said. "She healed me after the war tore me apart. When I come home, I was beat. I hated your ma and you kids, like you robbed me of something I could have been. And all the time I knowed you were all there was for me. For a long time, I didn't know what a rare gift that was. But the land slowly taught me gratitude. And gratitude, son, that's what makes a real life."

"I won't be beholden," Reid said quickly.

"No, it ain't like that. It's knowin' one day you got everything you need. Everything's there like a fallow field. And all you got to do is realize what is instead of what ain't. And you see there's something greater than you providing more than you probably deserve, waiting for you to quit worrying about the other fellow or better times, waiting for you to take hold of what you have and get on with what's before you."

Reid looked at the log rafters running across the roof. He could count the bare shingles between him and the sky. "It's too late for me, pa," he said grimly.

"Boy, that's just your emotions talkin'. You got whatever there is of time in your life. You got it now, like you ain't got yesterday, like you'll wish you had it next year or the year after."

"I'm goin' away, pa. If I stay, they'll catch me and put me in jail. I can start over somewhere else where I ain't known or wanted."

"You can do that, Pace," his father said wearily as he stood up. "How long you going to have to struggle to get a start somewhere else? What's going to keep you from turning again to thieving? If you make it honest, you'll still be in debt for what you done. And all the time'll be waste, boy. You already are a man of substance. All you have to do is open your fist long enough to receive the good."

"I won't take what I ain't earned," Reid said to his father's back.

"You always have," Pa Reid said softly. "You think simple receiving makes you less than another man. You'd rather be a thief and take it from him."

"Railroads and banks ain't men, pa," Pace said.

"No, they're just the little hopes of lots of little men," his pa said, and opened the door. "It takes a big man, Pace, to realize he's in debt to life and not holler or whine but be thankful and carry the debt with dignity and purpose. We are meant for receiving, son, and for passing the gifts along. Think on it. It takes some thinkin'."

"I ain't in debt to no man, nor will I bow in gratitude."

"Sure ya are, son. You're in debt to every man who ever wanted to be more than a poor starvin' animal and fought to be a man. They ain't always won, that's for damn sure, but they didn't let the coals burn plumb out. If you ain't thankful for that, you ain't the man I think you are. And you're in debt to whoever created everything. But you're mad 'cause you didn't make it. And be damned if you'll receive it. But you can't slap that hand away, son. It's too big, and it spreads itself too far. Inside, you know that, and you hate yourself for being so mean-spirited," Pa Reid said. He closed the door, sealing the thoughts in the room.

Lying in bed, Reid listened to his footsteps on the creaking stairs. "Shoot!" he said, and turned to the wall throwing his leg over the covers. "Shoot! Shoot! Shoot! This damn being laid up gives a man too much time to think."

Reid did have time to think. Some things became clear to him in the quiet room above the kitchen. Cole Dyer had set them up. He planned the robbery with full knowledge of the seven armed guards. He and the conductor took the money while the guards pursued the outlaws. He rode with the posse.

He didn't betray Reid to Blood because the hunt for him kept the deputy's mind away from him. Setting the young outlaws on Reid's trail was just more smoke. Reid's mind made a sudden leap as he remembered the firepower at Rhema Blood's cabin. Dyer had meant for them to kill him, shut his mouth for good. Again, he had sent others to do his work and take the consequences without dirtying his own hands.

Suddenly, Reid wanted his gun. Just feeling the cold, deadly instrument would sustain him until he could repay Dyer full measure for his pain and for the deceit. Reid looked across the room at his pistol hanging on the back of the chair. As he lay looking at the gun, he noticed the grip looked different. Reid struggled out from under the cover and hopped over to the chair. He drew the gun out. It lay well in his hand. But he knew instantly it was not his own. It was Cap Starr's. Reid knew the weapon well. He'd given it to Starr, had ordered the fancy grips with stars cut into them. Reid sat perplexed.

He retraced his journey back slowly. The last he'd handled the gun was at Rhema Blood's place. He saw himself there against the wall. His pistol and others were in the floor under the shooting slot. When Ruven Blood showed up, he knew he had to git. He reached into the floor and picked up a gun, but he never took his eyes off Rhema. Then he ran. He had taken Cap Starr's pistol instead of his own.

That was how he came to have the gun, but how had the gun come to be there? Reid thought back to the dugout saloon and the night Starr died. Before he covered Starr's face with the blanket, Jack Patrick took the pistol and belt off him. He wound the belt slowly around the holster and laid it on top of the blanket on Starr's chest. He and Roots and Reid sat in the wet-seeping room with Starr's body all night. That was the last Reid saw of the gun.

The pain of the night came back slowly over Reid. The three of them sat in that weeping room without talking for a long time. There were no words. Reid could not talk at all or even hear as he stared at the shrouded body. Patrick must have talked awhile before Reid began to listen.

"It was raining that night, too," Reid heard him say. "We rode into a little place between two creeks. We'd been shot to hell outside Evansville. Cap's little brother was killed. He had the kid draped over his horse. He was just a kid — fifteen, sixteen years old. We broke in the house. There was just a white woman and her colored woman. We made them feed us supper. Cap wouldn't eat. He found a bottle and kept after it while we ate.

"He laid the kid out in the parlor on a door we took down. It was awful to see him washing the kid, setting up the candles. We all just sat there around the body. The drinking didn't do Cap any good. Nothing could ease his hurt. Finally, he grabbed the woman and made her look at the boy's head. Whole side of his head was shot off. He took the woman upstairs then to the bedroom. I don't think he wanted her so much as he just wanted to get shut of the pain in him. The battle between those two went on all night. She wasn't easy handled. She was a match for Starr. Next morning, we buried the boy and rode off.

"Cap was ashamed of what he'd done to the woman. But once done, it could not be undone. She was a married woman, and her husband was off fighting. It bothered Cap more and more as the weeks and months passed. Sometimes he'd just sit for hours thinking. I don't reckon Cap Starr ever got over what he'd done. He'd broke some faith with himself and couldn't forgive it or forget it. He wasn't a man to hurt a woman or shame her.

"We raided up into Missouri for a spell," Jack Patrick said, getting up and walking about the room. "Got pretty close to St. Louis once or twice. But Cap's mind wasn't on his business. Finally, we were ordered back into Arkansas. Out around Van Buren, a federal patrol caught us. Arkansas was always unlucky for us. Cap and I was the only ones who got away. He was bad hurt, bleeding bad. We ran up and down creek beds all day. When he couldn't go no further, I found him a little dry place and prayed the rain would stop. And then the woman came. She and her black woman was looking for her lost lambs. She had a gun. She raised it to kill the captain. Boy, her hate for him was plain. I think he wanted her to pull the trigger.

"'Damn you for coming back,' she said. 'Damn you more for coming back hurt.' She put the gun down, and we got Cap on his feet. The black woman helped me carry him to the house. The woman hung back, didn't offer to help with the load. I figured she hated him too much. But when we got inside, I saw her condition. She was big with child. And she knew the healing arts well. But the strain of excitement brought on her time early. She had her baby — Starr's son — the next morning.

"She could never explain the child to her husband or the community. He went off and left her. Her convictions were strong against divorce or remarriage.

She became an outcast, she and the boy. They lived out there alone. She taught him school, for the town wouldn't take him. Knowing their struggle and shame, Starr's grief grew with the years. But the woman bore up. She raised the boy to be a strong, honest man. Starr wanted me to see to her, but she don't need nothing. The boy might like his things."

So Starr's gun had gone to Ruven Blood, the son of his hurt. Reid closed his eyes. Ruven Blood was Cap Starr's own son. "Shoot!" Reid said. Blood had been born in shame, ridiculed by good folks all his life. He'd turned out a man. He'd made a life out of his mess. Reid felt small and sorry. He'd made a mess out of his life.

★ ★ ★

In a few days, Reid had had enough of bed and his thoughts. His wounds had made him too vulnerable to too many voices and thoughts. He came to breakfast shakily with the help of a crutch but on both legs. After breakfast, he followed Matt out into the yard and watched him cut kindling.

"Pa's mellowed, ain't he?" Reid said.

"How's that?" asked Matt while he split the small log in half.

"I don't think he hates me so much anymore. He tried to give me some land," said Reid, poking at the ground with the crutch.

"We bought the Frazier place five years ago for you after he gave me this piece." Reid had heard his pa gave the home place to Matt. "We been workin' it ever since for you on shares. Puttin' your money in the bank every year," Matt said.

"You mean I got a farm and money in the bank all this time. Why didn't you tell me?"

"Why ain't you been home in five years, Pace?" asked Matt in response.

"Hell, I didn't feel welcome," Reid said.

"It was your own feelin', then," his

brother said. "We been lovin' you right along."

"Shoot!" said Reid. "Well, I'm goin' to blow the money and sell the farm. Serve you right for tryin' to help a worthless rat like me. Ain't nothing lower than me."

"You got a right to your opinion, brother," Matt said, splitting the kindling again. "But that don't mean it's right."

"Why'd you do it? To shame me more?"

Matt struck the ax in the big stump. "Look, Pace, you always took pa wrong 'cause he didn't fight back at bad times the way you wanted him to. You never once asked him why he was the way he was or tried to understand him. He could have gone off with those damned old Confederate outlaws you saw down by the creek. But he stayed. He stayed, Pace. And he found something — I ain't sure I understand what. He thinks he did wrong by you as a boy. He thinks he never took the time to teach you. He wants to make it up. He wants

198

to give you a clear choice between living as a man or an outlaw. This time, he wants you to really choose between being for something or against everything."

"Shoot!" Reid said. "I can't stand no more of this. I remember now why I went off. I can't see how it slipped my mind and I ever came back."

"Maybe 'cause you're too good a man to ride with men like that Michael you was talkin' about in your sleep."

Reid turned away, mumbling to himself, and hopped toward the barn. He opened the big door and smelled the scent of hay and oats and animals come forth like a lost memory found. He went into the hall down toward the cows and mules. A soft whinny greeted him. Reid hurried toward the piebald bay. He caught the big jaw to him and stroked the soft muzzle.

"Indian name of Thom Roots brought him in a while back," Matt said behind him. "You could always pick a good horse, Pace. Kind of an instinct."

"Yeah," Reid said quietly, almost to himself. "I never stole but one bad one, and I passed him along pretty quick."

Pace Reid was gone the next morning. He left the horse and the deed and the bankbook. He also left a note. "I have to pass along a bad horse," it said. "I've rode it a long time and will have some trouble getting it off my hands. But I hope to find a buyer in Fort Smith who will not want too much boot. Your son and brother, Pace Reid."

13

REID met Ruven Blood at the Huntsville depot. Reid sat on the bench in front of the little board and batten building and waited for Blood. The sheriff made no move to jail him because he had come in by himself without a gun or horse and had wired Fort Smith for the U.S. marshal. Besides that, Arkansas law had no jurisdiction in the Black Oak robbery in the Indian territory. Reid's reputation, however, had crossed the border. The town and its sheriff came down to see Reid go in. Reid was a famous son of the county now, having eluded the best of Parker's men for almost two months. In that time, country men were not always hard on a man who'd run crossways of the law. They took even an outlaw as a man, good or bad. Their condemnation fell gently on men like Reid, who hit the railroads or the hated government. But they were hard on the back shooters and sneak thieves who troubled the poor and helpless.

"How's your folks, Pace?" the sheriff asked. "I heard your pa was down with something but never got out that way before he was up again."

"My pa's fine, Sheriff Weems," Reid said, looking at the small, wiry old symbol of justice. He was different now, older, but Pace remembered how he was on election days and Fourth of July when he was a kid. Weems held the men in order with a loose but sure rein. Even when they were bad, he never forgot they were friends and neighbors.

"They sure have done a lot with that farm, your pa and Matt," Sheriff Weems said.

"They have done that," Reid said, trying to be agreeable in passing the time with the sheriff. "Sheriff, if you got business, you don't have to sit here with me. I ain't runnin' no more."

"I know that, Pace," Weems said. "I'd just like to sit here with you like your pa would if he could 'til the train comes in."

Ruven Blood rode in on the Bentonville train. As the train pulled into the depot, Reid saw the big man standing on the train steps with his coat pulled back over his sidearm. He looked cross all the way through, like a tired man does. Behind Blood was a second deputy. When Blood stepped down, Reid stood up. "You Pace Reid?" Blood asked.

"That's so," said Reid, looking the deputy marshal straight in the eye.

"You goin' of your own will?"

Reid nodded. "My own will," he said.

"Put out your hands," Blood said.

Reid hesitated. Sheriff Weems spoke. "He can't walk without a crutch. If you cuff him, he can't get around."

Blood turned to the small, indomitable

sheriff. "You vouch for this man, Sheriff Weems?"

"I've known Pace Reid all his life. He'll do what he says. He won't trouble you going in even without those handcuffs."

So Reid passed into the custody of the U.S. court on the Huntsville train platform. He walked into the car ahead of Ruven Blood and the other deputy. He sat down near the window. In the lantern lights of the station, he saw the sheriff sit down and push his hat back on his white hair. When Blood sat down, Reid felt trapped and sick for leaving. Every instinct in him cried out run, but Reid had given his word, and it held him tighter to the marshal than any chain could. The train chugged out of Huntsville, heading for Fort Smith. It was done, Reid thought. As the train passed the crossover road to the Reid farm, Pace saw two men sitting in a farm wagon, watching for the train. Neither Matt nor Pa Reid waved or gave any sign to the train, but Reid knew they were there. It was between them — a bridge for a badman.

Ruven Blood bought Reid his supper from a vendor on the train. "I ain't hungry," Reid said.

"Eat it, anyway, Reid," Blood said. "You need buildin' up before you see Judge Parker."

"Why'd Parker want to see me?" asked Reid. "I sure as hell ain't no big shakes as a robber."

"Small matter of fifty thousand dollars." Blood chewed his sandwich.

"Well, I ain't got it. You're as like to have it as me," Reid said, biting down on a sour pickle.

"Somebody's got it," the marshal said.

"Well, it ain't me, I can tell you that," said Reid.

"You think you know who?" asked Marshal Blood.

"I know I know who," said Reid softly.

"If you and Roots talk to the judge, the double-crosser has a good chance to go up to Detroit," Blood said.

"Has Roots come in?"

"By himself about a week ago," the marshal said.

"We rode a long way together," said Reid.

"You'll ride a long way further," Blood said, leaning back in the seat and pulling his hat brim over his eyes.

"You got a good horse," Reid said quietly.

"My saddle ain't much now," said Blood from beneath the hat. Reid looked at the other deputy. He wasn't sleeping.

Reid's arrival in Fort Smith took him by surprise. There was a little jail buggy waiting, and he got right off the train into it. He rode standing up beside Ruven Blood down the wide street from the tracks to the federal court and jail compound. Reid looked at the people standing in the street, staring.

"Hell, they seen lots worse than me," he said.

"You made us look bad, Reid. Folks

want to see a man who got out from under our noses five times." He held out his fingers.

"Five times?"

"At the train, in the squirrel woods, at Johny Jim's, out by the ferry crossing with the Ridge family, and at my mother's place," said Blood. "We haven't been that far behind you."

"That's plain enough," said Reid. "How come you didn't hit my pa's place?"

"Weems thought you ought to have a chance," said Blood.

"Shoot!" Reid said as they came in sight of the big red-brick courthouse. Reid's eyes drifted beyond it to the gallows as he and Blood climbed the wide stone steps. "Am I into it for shootin' that Ridge kid?"

"Be hard to tell whose bullet killed him, yours or his brother's," said Blood as he swung open the wide white door to the courthouse and jail.

There were papers to fill out and a lot of men Reid did not know. He was tired and weak, so he stretched out on a long bench outside Brizzolara's office. Brizzolara was the U.S. Commissioner. He decided whether a case went to court. As Reid reclined against the hard oak, he recognized one of the crowd. The man had a big nose and a big head and a big hat. Walter Goss, of the *Saint Louis Globe Democrat*, came toward him. As Reid's assistant on the Black Oak train, he'd seen Reid well. Being a newspaper man, he was not likely to forget. Reid sighed. The doors were clanking shut one by one.

"You robbed the train," Walter Goss said emphatically.

"I haven't denied it," said Reid without enthusiasm.

"What did you do with the loot?"

"I gave fifteen dollars and a gold watch to each of the others to bury me, but I didn't die, and I didn't take it back, either. I buried the sack by a log that I couldn't find again 'fore I was ninety-nine. I tried to give a black man some, but he would not have it. I took the grand sum net of twenty-five dollars, and I give it to a lady. That comes out to zero in my books," Reid said.

The reporter blew through his lips in a kind of snort. "Fifty thousand dollars! What did you do with that?"

Reid sat up. Goss jumped back. "I'm tired of hearing about that $50,000. It damn near got me killed too many times already, and I ain't seen it. If I had it, I'd admit it. I ain't. You got that. You go on, or I'll set the law dogs on you." The reporter went away. "Shoot!" said Reid, settling back. "Fifty thousand dollars!"

But Reid did not rest long. Cole Dyer emerged from Brizzolara's office. Their eyes met, and Dyer looked away. He almost caught a passing deputy's arm. "That's the man who stole my mule!" he said, pointing at Reid.

Reid's mouth fell open. "Why, you hypocrite, you false witness," Reid said, grabbing for Dyer just as Ruven Blood pushed him back on the bench.

"You know that man?" asked Blood.

"Why?" returned Reid suspiciously.

"He says you stole his mule," said Blood.

"I'll kick his ass," said Reid as Dyer got away, using the other deputy as a shield. "I'll be damned. I'll just be damned if he ain't got it for gall. He give me that mule to use. It damn near killed me to boot. Last I seen of it, it was headin' home."

"It never got there," said Blood, leading Reid toward the big cage that ran through three floors of the toughest outlaws of the frontier.

"Shoot!" said Reid. *I bet that damn snake sold it. Like ridin' a saw blade. I was damn near cut in two,* Reid thought as they walked. *It was so poor it might have just died.*

They took Reid's personal property and put him in the hospital ward, but his anger did not subside. He held on to it to keep his mind off the cold eternity sound of iron doors banging shut. "That snake!" he said, lying on the bunk. "Think's he's smart and safe, don't he?"

* * *

The new federal jail at Fort Smith costs fifty thousand dollars. The first prisoners moved in, in March of 1888, two years after the project began. There were three floor of cells — the first level for murderers, the second for robbers, and the third for whiskey peddlers and those receiving a one-year federal sentence. Each floor had its own water closet, which simplified housekeeping and made the jail a model. Indoor plumbing was a novelty to Reid. Sometimes, 266 men were packed into the seventy-two five-by-eight-feet cells and their hallways. Even early on, it was plain that crime was outdistancing the facilities provided to stop it. But the new jail was a hundred times better than the basement jail under the court. In that hole, there were no bunks, no gaslights, no toilets. There were just walls and cold, damp floors and desperate men.

After a few days, Reid joined Thom Roots in the thief's section of the jail. When Thom hammered on Reid's cage, it was like the joyful reunion of two old hunting dogs, shy and formal.

"You lived?" asked Roots.

"You damn betcha," answered Reid smartly. "What in hell are you doin' here?"

"Oh," said Roots, "I decided to get shut of the law. How about you?"

"Me?" said Reid. "I got a bad horse to pass along 'fore it kills me. How's this place work?"

"It ain't bad," said Roots. "The doctor'll be here in a minute to see who's sick. You're sick, Reid. You listen to him."

"I seen enough of him. I'm feelin' just fine," said Reid.

"You're lookin' pale," said the Indian. "But it's hard to tell with white folks what's natural and what ain't."

"Kiss my foot," said Reid, and he smiled.

"Breakfast is a tin cup of black coffee, half a loaf of bread, a piece of bacon fat, a little rice and sorghum 'lasses. Dinner and supper's always the same — slab of corn bread about this big." Roots held out his fingers about six inches. "There's some beef and one garden vegetable all in a quart pan. It ain't real tasty, but there have been times I'd have settled for less."

Reid's eyes narrowed, and his forehead furrowed into a frown. "You're grateful, ain't you, Thom?"

"Well," the Cherokee said, embarrassed. "It's a damn sight better than freezin' and starvin', Pace. I ain't recommendin' it to anyone, but it could be a damn sight worse."

"You're goin' to make it," said Reid flatly. "I can see you're goin' to make it out of here and back home."

"Hell, Reid," said Thom Roots, "I ain't killed nobody. I'm for sure goin' to get out of here after a spell."

"Yeah, I know," Reid said, "but you're goin' to have a life, too."

"Damn, Reid, are you funnyheaded again?"

"No, I can just see some things clear at the moment," said Reid, lying back on his bunk.

"What you said about the robbery?" asked Roots.

"Not much 'cept I was there and done it," said Reid.

"You said anything about who else was there?"

"Not yet. What you figure?"

"I figure to see it through and be a law-abiding man."

"You aim to speak against Dyer?" asked Reid.

"He's the thief, ain't he? Planned it and took the money, too."

"He says I stole his mule," said Reid. "You ever hear of me stealin' a mule?"

A deep laugh rumbled through Thom Roots. "Stole his mule, did you? I swear, Reid, what you've fell to is pitiful." Then Reid laughed, too, and the men went together to get their breakfast.

The weeks past slowly for Thom Roots and Pace Reid. They were men used to a free life, traveling about as the urge moved them. The strictures of the jail worried them and made them restless. They struggled to be amiable with the other prisoners and even the guards. At first, Reid even enjoyed the talk and companionship, but gradually he tired of the common robbers, for their talk was cheap and shallow. Reid turned more and more to the old friend Thom Roots.

"Why ain't you worried about the sheriffs?" Reid asked.

"'Cause they ain't important."

"The hell they ain't."

"Think about it, Pace. What can they do to us? Take the money? We ain't got it," the Cherokee said.

"They can slap our tails in a damn jail for ten years."

Thom Roots continued to smoke

contemplatively. The faint smoke of the cigarette rose lazily. "We ain't killed anyone. They can't hang us."

Reid's eyes drifted beyond Roots to the young outlaw lifting the mattress on Reid's bunk. "Not yet," he said, rising slowly. Reid made his way slowly and inconspicuously from the common pen toward his cell. He caught the boy coming out and slammed him against the bars. "What's your name, thief?" Reid demanded.

"Elton James," the boy sputtered.

"What you doin' in there around my gear?"

"Nothing. I wasn't doing nothing. Let me be," the boy said, and Reid let him go. The boy swung hard at Reid. Reid slapped his hand aside. Again and again, the boy tried to hit Reid as Reid slapped him about the corridor. Reid never closed his fist against the young hoodlum, nor did he stop his relentless pursuit.

"Guard!" the boy yelled desperately. "Guard! He's killing me. Guard!"

Reid slapped the boy hard against the wall and caught his jaw in one hand. "Shut up, punk," he said. "You listen to me, Elton James. Anything goes wrong any time around my gear and I'm comin' for you. You got that?"

The boy protested. "It won't be me. I ain't done nothing."

"I don't give a damn who done it, kid. I ain't in the judgement business. I'm in Retribution with a capital R." Reid grinned broadly. "Got that now?" He moved the boy's head up and down. As the guard appeared, he shoved the young outlaw. "Go call mama or grow up." The boy walked away, ignoring the guard. Reid smiled sweetly at the deputy. "Nice day, ain't it?"

Reid felt the frustration and restlessness growing in him as the days passed. In a cage, it was easy to forget the reasoning that had brought him to turn himself in. As he lay in the bunk at night, he tried to see what he'd gained or even thought he might have gained. "Thom," he said, "why'd you come in, give in to the bastards?"

"I give in years ago, when I let 'em set my course, Pace," the Indian said. "I don't want a life of running and hiding and getting drunk to forget I hate myself as much as them. I'm takin' my life back from 'em. I'm going to get free."

"You're plumb crazy, Indian. You're laying here in prison talkin' about getting free."

"Back in North Carolina, my grandpa had two buckets on his porch by the door. One was clear, cold spring water, and one was sippin' whiskey. There was a gourd dipper in each one. You had to drink whatever you took out or throw it on the ground. You never made another man drink your leavings. All the time I knew that old Indian and the men around him, I never seen one drunk or dry. But out here us Indians never leave a drop of drink in a fifty-cent bottle of Bust Head. What you think of that? Which of us is free men — that damned hardheaded

Cherokee who set his own limits or us defying the law?"

Reid thought about Roots' grandpa and the whiskey. "I reckon the old man was free," he said. "'Cause he chose for himself."

"Well, I'm choosin' for myself. I got two roads before me — outlawin' or jail. I'll be a free man in the tightest jail," said the Indian Thom Roots. Reid did not answer his friend but lay awake thinking through the long prison night.

In February, Ruven Blood came for Reid. He walked out of the cage with the aid of a cane. He went down the wide stairway past the desk guards, through the halls and confusion to Judge Parker's private chamber. Blood swung the door aside, and Reid stepped into the room. Blood did not follow but closed the door behind him, leaving Reid alone in the comfortably messy room.

Parker stood at the window. His attention was outside somewhere. He seemed not to even notice Reid at all. Reid waited, sensing that it was not just a man before him. Maybe it was the same feeling that made Blood and most of the other deputies always say 'Judge Parker' or 'the Judge' with a different inflection than regular speech. Maybe it was that Reid sensed that Parker was no longer a private man like himself.

Parker had taken on a different nature because of the great burden of law he carried for the people, people like Reid's pa and Matt. He might laugh at a joke or smoke a cigar like other men, but after a bit, he'd have to walk another road beyond other men's understanding. Standing there at the window smoking his cigar, even there, away from the high bench of judgement in the courtroom, he seemed imposing. There was a secret life inside him, an unshared mystery that had to do with the idea of justice, the truth beyond the petty and big laws of men in relation to each other.

"Take a seat, Mr. Reid," the Judge

said without turning from the great window. Reid found a hard oak chair in front of Parker's desk. "Deputy Blood says you've given yourself up." He turned to see Pace Reid nod his affirmation. "I do not know why you made your decision, but I know it is the right one." Reid suddenly felt it was more than right, that it was all right and he was safe. "You did not take much money for your trouble in the Black Oak robbery."

"I inconvenienced the railroads some," said Reid.

"They have never been my friends, either," said Judge Parker, coming toward his chair. "And that is why I work so hard to see they receive full benefit of the law and not my own feelings. That is why I need your help." Reid could not see how his help would mean anything to the Judge. "There were other men besides you and Thom Roots involved in robbing the train. Four men."

Five, thought Reid. Then he thought,

four besides me. The judge is on to something here. "I'd not want to draw other men into my decision to come in and confess," said Reid.

"The railroad wants its money returned. If not, it demands the robbers be made an example for others."

"Thom and I didn't get any money," Reid said, looking at his hands. "I just picked the passengers, and that was it."

"Why did you let the miner keep his savings?" asked Parker.

Reid looked up, startled by the Judge's knowledge of that detail. "He had a wife and little kids, and he'd worked hard for his wad."

"You are a just man, Mr. Reid. You weighed the matter and came down on the side of justice even though you were a thief. I want you to weigh something else now. There are men guilty of a crime that you have knowledge of. They are free, and they have committed a robbery. You may suppose they just robbed a train and

222

find that a small offense. But they have done much more than that. They have robbed society, all the honest men and women who get up tired and go back to hard labor and small pay — people like the miner and his wife — to earn their way. And robbery was not enough; they've mocked them, too, making fun of their efforts, rubbing salt in the bleeding wounds. I don't believe you are a man to rob and mock justice, Mr. Reid. But I believe you know such a man."

Reid looked squarely at the Judge. "I know the man, sir, but I'm not sure whether I want him caught just because of what he done to me or because of what he done to other folks."

The Judge rested his chin on his knuckles as he sat back thoughtfully in the chair. "Personal revenge would be unworthy of any man," he said.

Reid continued as the Judge seemed to be thinking. "There is an unwritten code among outlaws about telling on another man."

"When you gave yourself up, you accepted a new code that supersedes the old. You have become part of the compact, the great tradition of men working together to remove strife and contention from their midst in reasoned ways. You are united now with free and just men against thieves and destroyers," said Judge Parker. "Some people come before this court sure that our mission is to rob them and kill them. They are wrong. Our purpose is to protect. To protect the innocent from the predators. To protect the guilty from the emotional excesses of his victim. But when justice must decide between the innocent victim and the knowing violator, she must choose the innocent because that is good for the hopes of all men.

"It has become a game to rob justice, to pervert her intentions. It is no longer just the bad men who are mocking justice. It is the good men, or at least the legal men. The stewards of the temple are bartering and selling."

Reid looked intently at the judge, drawn to the phrases about good men and bad men. "Judge Parker, who do you figure a good man is? I been wondering a long time about the meaning of good and bad and whether there even was a meaning or just a shifting, floating thing a man can't stand on."

Judge Parker raised his white head and studied Reid. "I, too, have wondered, Mr. Reid. Every time I pronounce sentence on a man, I wonder. I suppose all justice revolves around the question of what is good or bad about an action and what circumstances temper the action — like the difference, say, between murder and self-defense. Both are killing. Killing is wrong. But we make exception for the man who kills by accident or in an effort to protect himself or his family from unprovoked attack lest we do another and greater injustice.

"We speak of 'intent' in the law business. By it we mean what was in a man's heart and mind when he committed an act. It is there in the heart and mind that good and evil lie. And it is the small and selfish and hurtful intents that catch a man up in evil. There is an instinct in people, some true North, that sorts it out finally. The people make their own heroes and villains around that little true center. You have the sure instinct of the people."

Reid sat still, thinking about Parker's words as the judge waited silently. "Look, Judge, I got off wrong in beginning my life. I went too much for the sparkle and show. I aimed to do everything in a big way, fast. I was impatient with steady men. I took 'em for dullards and cowards. They just never seemed to me to aim high enough." Reid thought about Matt and pa and Sheriff Weems. How they stood by him. "Hell, I been wrong. I get sick sometimes thinking how wrong I been. And I wonder why I couldn't see what Matt, my brother, saw. Why it took me so long to understand things. I mean, I thought I was so far ahead of everybody, and here I sit dead last. Still, I don't think I ever was a small or mean man." Reid fidgeted in the chair, unconsciously rubbing the numb leg. "I ain't going to tell you who all was in the Black Oak robbery. It wouldn't serve no purpose — they are family men. They never got near the train no way or seen any profit. And getting hold of them would do you no good, but it would hurt their people. The one who planned the robbery and got away with the money is Cole Dyer."

"Cole Dyer, who helped with the posse?" asked Parker.

"Helped misdirect 'em," Reid said.

"Mr. Reid, will you stand by this in open court?"

"I've made my choice, Judge Parker."

Parker sat up quickly and wrote on a pad in front of him. "If your testimony leads to the conviction of Cole Dyer, you shall go free on one stipulation."

"What stipulation?"

"That you never rob or commit any other criminal act again."

"You have my word on that," said Reid, and offered his hand. Parker stood up and took it, shaking Reid's hand firmly.

14

REID stood in front of the broken mirror, studiously combing his thick, dark hair into place. He wet the comb and slicked down a particularly unruly lock, then dabbed at it with his hands. Satisfied at last with the hair, he studied his image. The months of pain, running, and prison had taken what little fat he had. He was thin and gaunt. Being inside had made him pale, almost as pale as the faded blue eyes that gazed back at him. The shirt he wore was the one from Johny Jim's. It was the best he had. He buttoned it high at the collar. A buttoned collar made him feel formal and well turned out. As he left the little cell, he shined his boots against the back of his trousers. Thom Roots stood waiting. They walked to the main door. Ruven Blood was there.

Their day in court had come.

Before Reid reached the courtroom, his shirt was wet through from anxiety. He and Roots and Pood Ellis had all given themselves up and agreed to testify that Cole Dyer planned the Black Oak robbery. None of them ever mentioned Bill Russell. Russell's woman was sick, and he had seven children. Just living was load enough for him to bear.

"All rise. Stand on your feet," the crier said. Judge Parker came in in his heavy black robe.

"Oyez! Oyez! The honorable district court of the United States for the Western District of Arkansas, having criminal jurisdiction of the Indian territory, is now in session," called out Court Crier J. G. Hammersly. His voice carried over the small court room where farmers, businessmen and plain citizens stood holding their hats respectfully. The jury pool filled most of one section of the room. The rest were family of those whose cases might be called, some reporters, and curious folks who had come to see justice in action.

"The court is ready for the first case," announced Judge Parker without looking up from the papers he read before him at the great high desk.

"The United States versus Cole Dyer, Pood Ellis, Pace Reid, and Thom Roots. Charge: robbery," Hammersly said.

They started to call jurors. One by one, men from the jury pool were called. The jurors all came from Arkansas, which did not sit well with the citizens of the Indian Territory. It was not a jury of their peers for most of them. Some of the Indians thought white men got better treatment from white juries. Parker had raised jury pay from two dollars to three per day to get a better class of men. But even three dollars did not compensate a man for his time lost from work or business. Some begged off. Most came anyway, for justice's sake. Occasionally, a juror was seated. Some were sent away having admitted knowledge of the case, the defendants, or the lawyers. The Judge seemed to pay little attention to the empaneling. His private bailiff came in and out of the courtroom, bringing messages or papers and taking others away.

One of the prospective jurors came cautiously forward to the high desk where Parker sat. Parker looked up at the wiry farmer whose bald head gleamed with beads of sweat. He listened intently to the man's whispered words. Finally, the Judge nodded, and the man started away.

"Excuse Nathan Otwell. His cattle are out, and he must help his wife get them in before any damage is done," Judge Parker said in a voice that carried into the backmost corners of the court. Reid saw Nathan Otwell shrivel a little at the wide public announcement of his whispered conversation.

"Call Francis James Bolin," said Hammersly.

Francis James Bolin came forward slowly through the crowd, past the table of the lawyers and defendants. He stood stiffly in the railed-off box as the prosecutor, William Henry Harrison Clayton, centered on him. Clayton was a precise man, even in appearance. He was smaller than average, but with carriage and energy that contradicted his gray hair and small gold-rimmed spectacles. In fact, Clayton was an old soldier who'd fought at Antietam, Fredericksburg, and in the Battle of the Wilderness before he left the Union Army to teach tactics at a military school. He was a carpetbagger, like Parker himself, having come South from Pennsylvania after the war to occupy the defeated and impoverished land.

At first Clayton farmed a two-thousand acre plantation near Pine Bluff with his brothers. But he turned from that to the study of law. He became prosecutor for the First Judicial Circuit of Arkansas. He was its presiding judge when Grant appointed him U.S. Attorney for the Western District in 1874. Clayton was tenacious in the courtroom. He did his homework and stayed with a witness until he got what he wanted. That tactics study stood him well. Once, he prosecuted eighteen men for murder in one session of court and convicted fifteen. Clayton had energy for sure.

"Mr. Bolin," he said, "do you know any of the defendants in this case?"

"No, sir," said Bolin.

"Have you or any of your near relatives ever had business with any of the lawyers in this case?"

Bolin looked at the lawyer, H. Warren Bean, seated beside Dyer. "I heard if you're guilty, get him for your lawyer," said Bolin, nodding at Bean.

"I'll accept this witness," said Clayton with a chuckle.

"I won't. Dismissed," Bean said dryly as he stood up regally to his full height. "Dismiss the juror."

"Defense dismisses the juror," said

Parker. "Call the next juror."

Reid focused idly on Bean as the morning wore on. Physically Bean was impressive. His clothes were custom-made of the finest materials. His coats were cut in the claw-hammer fashion. He carried a silver-headed cane. Among the citizens of the frontier, Bean clearly was the dandy. Reid watched him examining the jurors. Somehow the coat grated against Reid. And Bean came to personify a great skreaking jaybird as he strutted across the old bare boards of the room. He just overpowered men in the box with his size, personal confidence, and voice.

Bean was the star of Parker's court. His record against the court was outstanding. In the murder cases he specialized in, convictions meant nothing. Bean went over Parker's head to the president or supreme court any time he lost in Fort Smith. The distant guardians of justice were easily persuaded of Parker's errors, especially with the growing railroad lobby against him and the Eastern public's outcry against the notorious 'Hanging Judge'. Bean was a sophisticated man in the law business. He knew all the holes in the fence and used them.

Reid slumped further in his chair. With Bean for his defense, Dyer's guilt might not be so obvious. When the last juror was seated, Reid felt soggy and exhausted.

"Stand up," someone beside Reid said, and Reid stood.

"How do you plead to the charge of robbery at Black Oak switch?" asked Parker.

"I done it," said Reid.

"Say, 'guilty, your honor'," the lawyer said.

"Guilty, your honor," Reid said. Thom Roots and Pood Ellis also pleaded guilty in front of the jurors and the official record.

"And you, Cole Dyer, how do you plead?" asked Parker of the final man.

"My client pleads *not guilty*," said

H. Warren Bean.

"I asked the defendant," said Parker.

"Not guilty," Dyer said. "I'm an innocent man."

The lie was what the jury heard as the men sat down raking their chairs into place. Reid had a great urge to smack Dyer across the mouth. "Innocent man, my rear end," said Reid. Thom Roots touched his arm, and Reid looked back at the Judge.

"Gentlemen of the jury," Parker said, "three of the defendants — Pood Ellis, Pace Reid, and Thom Roots — voluntarily surrendered themselves and have pleaded guilty before this court. They have made full confessions of their parts in the train robbery at Black Oak switch. And their confessions will be used by the prosecution as evidence against Cole Dyer."

The trail began then in earnest — Bean against Clayton and Judge Parker. It was more than a fair match, with Bean dominating the witnesses and jurors in front of Reid's eyes. Ellis crumbled under Bean's examination. By the time he finished with him, Ellis was not sure even if he had been at the switch. Thom Roots was silently resistant to Bean.

"Are you a thief?" Bean asked Roots.

"I was a thief," said the Indian.

"You *were* a thief and robber," said Bean loudly, turning his back to Thom and facing the jury. "For many years. In fact, you've also run whiskey. Is that so?"

"It is so."

"When you carried whiskey and a deputy or agent stopped you and asked if you carried ardent spirits, did you admit your guilt?"

"No," said Thom.

"You lied?" asked Bean. Roots nodded. "Speak up, Mister Roots."

"I lied," said Thom, looking down.

"Shoot!" said Reid to himself.

But Bean was not through with the Cherokee. "Why did you lie?"

Thom Roots looked up at Bean. "It was my business. To admit whiskey peddling would have meant a fine or jail."

"You stood to gain by your lie, then. By lying on Cole Dyer, won't you get less time in jail?" asked Bean.

Clayton came to his feet, "Objection!"

"Sustained," said the Judge.

"Very well," said Bean. "We are satisfied the jury knows this Indian for what he is, a thief and *liar*." The word 'liar' rang through the courtroom. Reid's mouth set hard at the insult to Thom Roots.

Reid himself was next called to the stand. He felt awkward and ill at ease. His apprehension had grown steadily as Bean called witnesses and cross-examined others. The palms of his hands were wet, and he rubbed them on his pants as he sat down. Clayton led Reid through a recital of the facts of the robbery, then finally turned him over to Bean.

"You're Pace Reid?" asked Bean casually.

"That's what I said," answered Reid.

"You admit robbing the train at Black Oak switch?"

"I do," said Reid.

"You *say* that Cole Dyer helped you?"

"That's right," Reid said.

"Where was Mr. Dyer that night at the switch?"

"He never showed up," said Reid.

"Oh, yes, I remember now you said he planned the robbery for you. How exactly did he do that?"

"He come to Catoosa where we were playing cards. After a while, we had a few drinks, and he said he knew a man in Dallas who knew when big money was shipped. This man in Dallas would tell him things, and a man could rob the train then, when he got the information."

"Did Mr. Dyer bring you that information later?"

"He did."

"His friend would have had *all* the information, wouldn't he?"

"I guess so."

"Dyer would have known about the seven armed guards. Did he mention that?"

"No, he sure as hell did not mention that."

The Judge said, "You're in a court of law, Mr. Reid." Reid nodded.

"Would you have held up the train if you'd known about the guards?"

"No, I sure as h — " Reid remembered the Judge's admonition. "No, I wouldn't."

"Did Mr. Dyer ride with the posse after the robbery, provide horses for them? I believe several deputy U.S. marshals have testified to that fact."

"That's so."

"Isn't it also conceivable that Dyer was in effect acting before the robbery as an agent for the railroad's interest in baiting a trap for the thieves who habitually rob and steal?"

"Damn," said Reid shouting. "He's a thief, a crook, a double-crosser, and you're sayin' he's an honest man."

Judge Parker rapped the hammer

down hard. "Enough of that."

Clayton was standing at the table. "Judge Parker, Mr. Bean has led this witness into a false conclusion that is unsubstantiated by any evidence showing Dyer acted as an agent of the railroad or the law."

Bean turned to the jury. "An undercover agent does not have papers saying he is an agent. Nor does a good citizen in hope of doing a good service require affidavits," he shouted above Clayton.

Parker pounded the gavel again and again, creating more chaos as the lawyers verbally flew at each other. Reid saw Dyer was smiling at the table. Reid stood up and started for the man. "Get him," yelled Bean. "He's out to get Cole Dyer."

The marshals grabbed Reid, who was still not swift of foot. They held him, but he didn't fight anymore. Reid had seen the case turn under him like a loose saddle. He looked up at Parker and saw the truth in the Judge's eyes, also. They'd been too sure. Three witnesses against Cole Dyer had failed to stop H. Warren Bean. Reid sat down slowly. The summations were masterful. Clayton struck every point made by Bean again and again. But Bean had created the little gnawing doubt that ate away justice from Cole Dyer. The men who left the jury box saw three admitted thieves out to get an honest man who had helped the law in every way.

It was a kind of miracle of foolishness. Dyer had planned it all. Dyer planned the robbery knowing the guards would go for the men confronting them. In the confusion, he lifted the $50,000 and got away. Not far. He didn't have to go far to get away. Reid sighed. It was masterful. Dyer left the courthouse a free man.

Reid and his friends returned to the jail. Reid threw his cane the length of the hall, but he knew it did no good. By the time he had limped down after it, all the anger was gone, drained away. He limped back to stand by Roots at the window. Outside, Bean and Dyer were laughing in the yard, enjoying their victory. They shook hands with men leaving the courthouse, men from the jury. Roots' black eyes never left the scene. "This," he said almost in a whisper, "this is the test."

Three days later, the three confessed thieves stood again before Parker. The Judge seemed tired. He sat for a long moment looking at them. "You are guilty of the robbery of a train at Black Oak switch in the Creek Nation. The law, therefore, sentences you to five years." Reid's and Root's jaws set. Five years was a long, hard time for a robbery that netted them nothing but pain and trouble. But both stood straighter, determined to see their bargain through. "You surrendered yourselves. You have been incarcerated since that time. During this time, you have been cooperative and model prisoners. Your accomplice has not served one hour. I therefore suspend your sentences to the time served with the stipulation you report to this court each year on the first day of September for the next five years. See the clerk for the proper papers." Parker returned to his papers as the men went away.

Reid stayed behind in the empty, twilight courtroom. Parker looked up. "I'm sorry it turned out this way," Reid said. "Cole Dyer was as guilty a man as was ever entertained here at Fort Smith. But you've been more than fair to me, sir. I bear you no ill feelings. As for the jury, I've been blind, too — blindest when I thought I was being my best. I'll be a mite more careful from here on. I reckon justice was best served in me seein' that, Judge." Reid turned away then and went down the hall to Stephen Wheeler's office. He shook hands with Ruven Blood and thought Cap Starr would have been proud of the big deputy. He was the good in the old badman. "Say howdy to your ma for me," he said.

He and Thom Roots left the prison together. Standing on the porch, they looked out across the yard toward the brick perimeter wall. The sun was a bright orange ball in the late-afternoon sky. Judge Parker and the little hangman, Maledon, were almost to the gate.

"Where to, Thom?" asked Reid.

"The Judge is going home. Think I will, too," said the Cherokee. "Be seein' ya, old friend." Then Roots stepped off the porch and followed the Judge and Maledon into the long shadows.

Reid sighed as he leaned against a post. He looked around, fixing the jail, the prison, the lessons learned in his mind. Across the yard, in the opposite direction from the city gates, stood the big gallows — the Gates of Hell. His eyes fell at last on the worn emblem of the scales of justice on the doorknobs. Reid stood a long time just looking and thinking. A precarious balance, he thought. Life has a precarious balance.

Some good. Some bad. He wondered suddenly if in his case those scales had not been tipped by some great unseen thumb to give a different measure. He realized suddenly that he was a lucky man. He smiled. Gratitude had at last overtaken Pace Reid as he walked slowly toward the city gate.

Author's Note

A new force in Western writing, C. H. HASELOFF lives in Springdale, Arkansas, but her roots stretch across into Texas. This unique background links the rich heritage of the frontier and the South into excitingly different Westerns. One of the most interesting locales of western history, Fort Smith, site of Judge Parker's Court, is a short morning's drive down the road.

★ ★ ★

Fort Smith sat on the precipice of civilization. A step across the river, or even a few hundred yards behind the Federal Court House to the infamous Coke Hill, brought the lawmen into a twilight world of unbelievable jeopardy. Sixty-five deputy marshals died during Parker's twenty-one years at Fort

Smith. They rode over 74,000 square miles, the largest legal jurisdiction in U.S. history, for the extravagant fee of six cents a mile one way. They paid their own and their prisoners' expenses and hoped for reimbursement.

I'm so tired of hearing about the brutality of Parker and his men. The simple fact is that killing a prisoner meant loss of all fees and the personal expense of burial, hardly incentives to murder of prisoners. The actions of these officers in bringing acts of treachery and butchery to justice is phenomenal even today. Parker himself was in the forefront of prison reform. His efforts led to the building of the new jail that replaced Hell on the Border. However, in his opposition to the railroads' efforts to divest the Indians of their common lands, he ran against powerful enemies in Washington who slowly but steadily eroded his power and built the myth of the Hanging Judge.

The stereotypical portrayal in films and books of Judge Parker is a terrible injustice in itself. Parker was a man of compassion and great personal character. He did not enrich himself in public office. He served. That he was maligned and his court reduced to impotence did not prevent him from carrying out his duty.

Parker's philosophy was simple. He believed that the surety of punishment not its severity stopped crime. For fourteen years the evildoers that came to his court had no appeal. Once found guilty, their punishment was certain. The death penalties that he hammered down were dictated by the law and by the belief that if the guilty went free, the innocent were mocked.

Fort Smith has a fascinating history that has been obscured by a cloud of dust from another time. Going back, seeing through the eyes of Parker's time, has taught me much about my own. That is one of the privileges afforded writers. In the next few years, I will write often of Fort Smith because there the great issues of law, men and civilization fought for resolution.

FIGHTING RAMROD
Charles N. Heckelmann

Most men would have cut their losses, but Frazer counted the bullets in his guns and said he'd soak the range in blood before he'd give up another inch of what was his.

LONE GUN
Eric Allen

Smoke Blackbird had been away too long. The Lequires had seized the Blackbird farm, forcing the Indians and settlers off, and no one seemed willing to fight! He had to fight alone.

THE THIRD RIDER
Barry Cord

Mel Rawlins wasn't going to let anything stand in his way. His father was murdered, his two brothers gone. Now Mel rode for vengeance.

HELL RIDERS
Steve Mensing

Wade Walker's kid brother, Duane, was locked up in the Silver City jail facing a rope at dawn. Wade was a ruthless outlaw, but he was smart, and he had vowed to have his brother out of jail before morning!

DESERT OF THE DAMNED
Nelson Nye

The law was after him for the murder of a marshal — a murder he didn't commit. Breen was after him for revenge — and Breen wouldn't stop at anything . . . blackmail, a frameup . . . or murder.

DAY OF THE COMANCHEROS
Steven C. Lawrence

Their very name struck terror into men's hearts — the Comancheros, a savage army of cutthroats who swept across Texas, leaving behind a bloodstained trail of robbery and murder.

DONOVAN
Elmer Kelton

Donovan was supposed to be dead. Uncle Joe Vickers had fired off both barrels of a shotgun into the vicious outlaw's face as he was escaping from jail. Now Uncle Joe had been shot — in just the same way.

CODE OF THE GUN
Gordon D. Shirreffs

MacLean came riding home, with saddle tramp written all over him, but sewn in his shirt-lining was an Arizona Ranger's star.

GAMBLER'S GUN LUCK
Brett Austen

Gamblers seldom live long. Parker was a hell of a gambler. It was his life — or his death . . .

McALLISTER ON THE COMANCHE CROSSING
Matt Chisholm

The Comanche, McAllister owes them a life — and the trail is soaked with the blood of the men who had tried to outrun them before.

QUICK-TRIGGER COUNTRY
Clem Colt

Turkey Red hooked up with Curly Bill Graham's outlaw crew. But wholesale murder was out of Turk's line, so when range war flared he bucked the whole border gang alone . . .

CAMPAIGNING
Jim Miller

Ambushed on the Santa Fe trail, Sean Callahan is saved by two Indian strangers. But there'll be more lead and arrows flying before the band join Kit Carson against the Comanches.

FARGO: PANAMA GOLD
John Benteen

With foreign money behind him, Buckner was going to destroy the Panama Canal before it could be completed. Fargo's job was to stop Buckner.

FARGO:
THE SHARPSHOOTERS
John Benteen

The Canfield clan, thirty strong were raising hell in Texas. Fargo was tough enough to hold his own against the whole clan.

PISTOL LAW
Paul Evan Lehman

Lance Jones came back to Mustang for just one thing — revenge! Revenge on the people who had him thrown in jail.

ARIZONA DRIFTERS
W. C. Tuttle

When drifting Dutton and Lonnie Steelman decide to become partners they find that they have a common enemy in the formidable Thurston brothers.

TOMBSTONE
Matt Braun

Wells Fargo paid Luke Starbuck to outgun the silver-thieving stagecoach gang at Tombstone. Before long Luke can see the only thing bearing fruit in this eldorado will be the gallows tree.

HIGH BORDER RIDERS
Lee Floren

Buckshot McKee and Tortilla Joe cut the trail of a border tough who was running Mexican beef into Texas. They stopped the smuggler in his tracks.

SUNDANCE: SILENT ENEMY
John Benteen

A lone crazed Cheyenne was on a personal war path. They needed to pit one man against one crazed Indian. That man was Sundance.

LASSITER
Jack Slade

Lassiter wasn't the kind of man to listen to reason. Cross him once and he'll hold a grudge for years to come — if he let you live that long.

LAST STAGE TO GOMORRAH
Barry Cord

Jeff Carter, tough ex-riverboat gambler, now had himself a horse ranch that kept him free from gunfights and card games. Until Sturvesant of Wells Fargo showed up.

BRETT RANDALL, GAMBLER
E. B. Mann

Larry Day had the choice of running away from the law or of assuming a dead man's place. No matter what he decided he was bound to end up dead.

THE GUNSHARP
William R. Cox

The Eggerleys weren't very smart. They trained their sights on Will Carney and Arizona's biggest blood bath began.

THE DEPUTY OF SAN RIANO
Lawrence A. Keating and
Al. P. Nelson

When a man fell dead from his horse, Ed Grant was spotted riding away from the scene. The deputy sheriff rode out after him and came up against everything from gunfire to dynamite.

WOLF DOG RANGE
Lee Floren

Will Ardery would stop at nothing, unless something stopped him first — like a bullet from Pete Manly's gun.

DEVIL'S DINERO
Marshall Grover

Plagued by remorse, a rich old reprobate hired the Texas Trouble-shooters to deliver a fortune in greenbacks to each of his victims.

GUNS OF FURY
Ernest Haycox

Dane Starr, alias Dan Smith, wanted to close the door on his past and hang up his guns, but people wouldn't let him.

GUNSLINGER'S RANGE
Jackson Cole

Three escaped convicts are out for revenge. They won't rest until they put a bullet through the head of the dirty snake who locked them behind bars.

RUSTLER'S TRAIL
Lee Floren

Jim Carlin knew he would have to stand up and fight because he had staked his claim right in the middle of Big Ike Outland's best grass.

THE TRUTH ABOUT SNAKE RIDGE
Marshall Grover

The troubleshooters came to San Cristobal to help the needy. For Larry and Stretch the turmoil began with a brawl and then an ambush.

FARGO: MASSACRE RIVER
John Benteen

The ambushers up ahead had now blocked the road. Fargo's convoy was a jumble, a perfect target for the insurgents' weapons!

SUNDANCE: DEATH IN THE LAVA
John Benteen

The Modoc's captured the wagon train and its cargo of gold. But now the halfbreed they called Sundance was going after it . . .

HARSH RECKONING
Phil Ketchum

Five years of keeping himself alive in a brutal prison had made Brand tough and careless about who he gunned down . . .